*Erik Torsten does not fit into Clarette Vanderpool's plan for her life. . .but God's plans are full of surprises.*

The water pooled deeper at a curve farther down the hillside. It was now up to her shins. Seeing something sparkling down in the water, she released his hand to step over to investigate. "What could it be?" she asked.

"Probably a crystal of some sort."

As she moved, she stepped on a flat stone that was slippery with moss and felt herself falling, but Erik's arms were immediately around her. "You'd better watch your step," he said, placing his large hand at her waist and pulling her to him. His words were a warm whisper on her cheek. Before she could answer, his lips came down ever so gently on hers.

**NORMA JEAN LUTZ** began her professional writing career in 1977 when she enrolled in a writing correspondence course. Since then, she has had over 200 short stories and articles published in both secular and Christian publications. She is also the author of five published teen novels.

**Books by Norma Jean Lutz**

HEARTSONG PRESENTS
HP41—Fields of Sweet Content
HP57—Love's Silken Melody
HP90—Cater to a Whim
HP121—The Winning Heart
HP155—Tulsa Tempest

# Tulsa
# Turning

*Norma Jean Lutz*

Heartsong Presents

*To Kerry and Tanya: My loving son and his beautiful wife. A "double-blessing" from the Lord.*

*To all those who know Tulsa well, and those who may remember the infamous 1921 race riot: thank you for allowing me the liberty of moving places, adjusting events, and adding people in order to tell Clarette's story.*

**A note from the Author:**
*I love to hear from my readers! You may write to me at the following address:*

Norma Jean Lutz
Author Relations
P.O. Box 719
Uhrichsville, OH 44683

ISBN 1-55748-873-8

**TULSA TURNING**

*Cover illustration by Brian Bowman.*

PRINTED IN THE U.S.A.

# one

Clarette Fortier stepped from the shadowy subway kiosk into brilliant May sunshine. Her heels clicked on the New York sidewalk as she threaded her way through the early morning go-to-work crush on Sixth Street. The highest windows on the soaring skyscrapers captured golden glints of sunlight and reflected down into the canyon where she stood waiting for the signal light to change.

A fat bus bulging with passengers chugged by, leaving a cloud of smelly exhaust. A horse-drawn vegetable vendor clip-clopped along the street's slow-lane. Cabbies shouted at the slower vehicles ahead of them, and blasting horns cut through the air. Clarette felt the city's pulse throb in the cement beneath her feet. Firming her cloche hat tighter on her dark, bobbed hair, she hurried across the street when the signal turned green.

A window dresser in a department store window struggled to set aright a demure blond mannequin with a boyish figure. The smiling, heavy-lidded statue was clad in a flapper dress of pink silk with row upon row of swishing fringes. No doubt the silk had come from one of her father's warehouses, Clarette thought. The pink-fringed number would be perfect for a night of dancing at the Dixie Club in Harlem. As she stopped for a moment to watch the mannequin be secured into place, she was painfully aware of her own plain gray suit.

The drab suit was the price she paid for working in the newsroom at the *New York American*. A price she willingly paid, she reminded herself.

"No cutesy, leggy numbers in my newsroom," Sid Epstein had barked at her the day he'd hired her. "I don't want these hot-headed men ogling over no dame." The thick stogie had rolled from one side of his mouth to the other as he'd talked. "They gotta keep their minds on the job. What minds they got."

He had looked with reproof at the raspberry crepe she'd worn that day. It had been the longest dress hanging in her closet at the time. But Sid had hired her and given her a chance to be a reporter. With great reservations—but he had given her a chance. She had promptly gone out and purchased three plain, straight-cut, gray suits. She called them her "work uniforms," a joke that delighted her roommate Herta.

On days when Clarette knew she would be out working on an assignment, she wore her knickerbockers and oxfords. Poor Grandmother Fortier would have fainted dead away if she had lived to see the day women wore trousers on the street, but Clarette thought 1921 was an exciting time to be alive.

She turned from the window to continue her walk down Sixth toward Broadway—but not before the window dresser gave her a bold wink. She smiled and winked back, then giggled at the look on his face.

She had not walked far when she saw through the crowd a lean, ginger-colored boy running toward her, his shoe-shine box banging against his side at each step. A man's discarded fedora was mashed on his head, and his long, thin legs sprinted expertly through the throng. *Shanks*, Clarette thought to herself, *is usually at Grand Central this time of morning; something must be amiss for him to be headed this direction.*

"Miss Clarie, Miss Clarie," he called when he caught sight of her. "I gots one, Miss Clarie. I gots a tip for you."

She slowed her pace and moved closer to the buildings where the foot traffic was lighter. Shanks came toward her at a dead run, and she feared for a moment that he'd not stop before he bowled into her. "I been looking for you, Miss Clarie. I gots you a good one."

He stopped directly in front of her, his brown face shiny with sweat. No telling how far he'd run.

"Good morning, Shanks. Aren't you missing the best time for customers at the station?"

He nodded, pulled off his hat, and clutched it to his heaving chest. "Yes'm. But I gots a tip for you."

Clarette had never regretted buying breakfast for this boy one morning a few months ago. He'd been a loyal friend ever since. His name, he had told her, was Spindle-Shanks. At least that's what everyone called him. She had never asked if there was a last name, and she had quickly shortened the name to Shanks.

She glanced around to see if any of the men from the newsroom were nearby. "It must be something hot for you to leave your money-making post."

He nodded. "A raid, they said."

"The Feds?"

"Uh-huh. The ones what's been taking shines most every morning and talking all the time about who's next."

She shook her head. "Sorry, Shanks. Good try, but a speakeasy raid is old news. There must be a dozen every night."

"This don't be no jive joint, Miss Clarie. They done got 'em a rumrunner. Out there." He pointed a long finger in the general direction of the Atlantic Ocean. "Some fella from the islands. They say they been waiting to get him."

"You don't say." She pulled out a notebook and pencil from her bag. "Now that *would* make a great story." She scribbled the name of the pier and a few other details as he described them.

Pulling a coin from her purse, she tossed it to him, and he expertly caught it. "This won't cover all the shines you missed, but it's the best I can do."

"Don't matter, Miss Clarie. I's glad to help." With a quick nod, he smashed the old fedora on his head, flashed her a bright smile, and disappeared through the crowd.

Jamming the pen and paper back in her bag, she wondered

how she could nab this story with no interference. Sid seemed to think she needed a watch dog each time she went out. What she desperately needed was a story all her own. Like this one. She quickened her step as she neared the *American* office building.

The rumrunner Shanks had mentioned must be McDow, the one with the ninety-foot schooner who easily did business outside the twenty-five-mile limit. Smaller runners went out to his floating bootleg store and paid fine prices for the whiskey brought up from Nassau. The Feds must have something new going. Or a trick to get McDow further inland. She wanted to be there when they towed his ship into port.

She breezed through the revolving door of the *American* building and into the grand marble-and-brass lobby. Heavy aromas of sausage and pastrami came from the little sandwich shop next to the lobby. Mr. Fabiano waved and nodded to her as she dashed past his door.

The dial above the elevator showed she would have a wait. Her heart was thudding as she thought how she would present this to Sid.

"Say, Fortier. What's the hurry? You were flying down the Sixth so fast, I couldn't catch up."

She looked over and saw her co-worker, Hank Maxwell. "So why'd you try?" she snipped at him.

He shrugged and glanced up at the dial. "Sure seems like a big hurry just to get to work."

"I like my work." Hopefully, Hank hadn't seen her chatting with Shanks. She wanted to keep her sources to herself.

"She likes her work," he mocked. "Mm-mm. Such a dedicated little thing. A dame in the newsroom. Cripes. You women get to vote, now you want our jobs."

Clarette wouldn't allow herself to answer. This wasn't how she would make it in the newspaper business—by winning little tiffs with two-bit fellows like Hank Maxwell.

The grate on the elevator door clattered open. "Mornin'," greeted the elevator operator. The young dark-skinned girl knew most of the newsroom people well enough not to have to ask for floor numbers.

On the eighth floor, Hank pushed ahead of Clarette into the newsroom, not bothering to hold the door. But she hadn't expected him to. He'd informed her on the day she was hired that if she wanted to work like a man, she'd be treated like one. His frail mind had never grasped the possibility that she could be a woman and still be a crack reporter. But he'd soon learn.

She went straight to her desk, sat down, and pulled papers from the basket to look over. Although she wanted to rush in and ask Sid for the assignment on the raid, she'd have to play it cool to keep Hank from getting suspicious. If he thought for a moment she had a lead, he'd want to be right in the middle of it.

She watched Hank out of the corner of her eye. The moment he moved to the far side of the room, immersed in conversation with another reporter, she grabbed the opportunity to slip into Sid's office. She took papers with her just in case Hank was looking.

Sid's answer to a knock was never, "Come in." Instead, he always called, "Yeah, what do you want?" The first few times she had been terrified, but she had learned now not to let him intimidate her. She stepped in and closed the door behind her.

"Sid," she said, "I have an inside news tip." Sid's cigar moved in his mouth, but he didn't look up from his desk. Her palms felt clammy. He might not believe her. Or he might believe her but not let her take the story. She plunged on. "I've learned that McDow's rum-running schooner is being raided this very morning, and that the Coast Guard will be bringing him into port. That is if there isn't a fight."

Sid looked up at last and hooked the cigar between his fingers. "Now where would a nice little lady like you hear a thing like that?" His gray eyes studied her under craggy eyebrows.

"Can I take the story, Sid?"

"How reliable is your contact?"

"Solid." Shanks kept his ears open, and he wouldn't tell her anything that wasn't true. Of that much she was sure.

"Even if it's true, they may have to chase McDow all the way to Nassau to catch him."

"Maybe. But maybe they'll surprise him. They have his accomplice in custody in North Carolina, and he doesn't know they have the goods on him. Maybe they'll bring him in quick and easy."

"You got a whole load of scoop, don't you, Miss Fortier?" He pronounced it Forty-air. Perhaps she should have made up a new name rather than taking her mother's maiden name to use—something simple and easy, like Jones.

"I have enough." She let him think on it a minute. He never offered her a chair, and she tried not to shift from one foot to the other. "Will you let me take it?" she asked at last when she could keep silent no longer.

"It's a long shot."

"You're a gambler. If nothing turns up by noon, I'll get back here and still have that society article ready for press time." She held her breath.

"I guess I got nothing to lose. Maybe it's a lead the *Times* don't know about yet."

She didn't answer. She hoped the lead was an exclusive, but she couldn't be certain. "Time's wasting, Chief."

He waved the cold cigar at her. "Go on. Go sniff it out. If it comes to anything, get up-close photos. If they're any good, we might use them in the rotogravure section of the Sunday magazine."

"Yes, sir." Excitement exploded inside her. She turned to the door.

"Miss Fortier?"

"Yes?"

"Better take Maxwell with you. The waterfront's no place for a lady. Even in daylight."

"But Sid. . ."

"Get on out of here. Time's wasting."

Her excitement was gone. She would have rather taken one of the young cub reporters than Hank Maxwell.

She grabbed her Graflex camera from beneath her desk, along with the bag loaded with boxes of cut film. Hank was at the water cooler. "Hank," she called. All heads turned, including Hank's. She walked toward the door. "Grab your hat. Chief wants you to come with me." If she was going to have to put up with him, she'd make it as hard on him as possible.

She could hear him groaning, "With a dame? Me? Why me?"

His questions were met with catcalls from his buddies: "Have a good time, Maxie." "Don't get lost." "All work and no play, you know!"

Clarette nearly reached the elevator before he came pounding up beside her, fuming. "What's up? Why didn't Sid brief me?"

"I guess he didn't want to waste time." In the elevator she quickly told him bits and pieces, but not all the story. She was tempted to transfer the bulky bag of film to his shoulder, but she resisted the impulse.

In the lobby she nearly ran headlong into Mr. Samuel Meikle, one of her father's business associates. She turned away just in time. She could just imagine his boisterous greeting: "Why, Clarette Vanderpool. Whatever are you doing here at the *American?* And with a camera?" That's all she would need to lose everything she'd worked so hard for this year. Sooner or later it was bound to happen, but she was determined to forestall the inevitable as long as possible.

On the street, now warmer in the near-summer sunshine, she stepped out to hail a cab.

"Hey, Fortier," Hank growled. "Wait just a minute. I ain't

gonna pay for no cab just to follow you down to the pier on a wild goose chase."

"Nobody asked you to. Follow in a bus." She bounded toward the cab that was slowing, wishing she had on her oxfords. "Pier sixteen," she told the cabby. "And hurry."

Hank hesitated on the curb momentarily, then jumped in beside her. "Dames," he muttered.

He was a different Hank when they saw police swarming around pier sixteen. "Would you look at that," he muttered. Clarette smiled inwardly as he automatically pulled money from his pocket to pay the cabbie.

Within minutes, they were watching the Coast Guard cutter smoothly towing in the sleek, twin-masted *Artemis*. Young Shanks had been right. She'd buy him a steak and eggs breakfast in the morning. She saw a couple of other reporters, but none she recognized. Maybe she really did have a scoop.

Suddenly, Hank was in charge. "Tell you what. Since this was your story, you head on down and try to get a statement from McDow or one of his boys." He pointed down the pier. "I'll nose around here and talk to the police. Some officer must be in charge of this deal." If she'd been thinking more clearly, she would have known not to trust him an inch. But his plan sounded fair.

The quiet harbor water sloshed softly at the sides of the boats, and the warm air was heavy with the smells of fish and salt water. Clarette moved as near the end of the pier as possible and watched as the uniformed Coast Guard soldiers herded the crew of the *Artemis* down the gangplank onto the dock. Boldly, Clarette closed in with her camera. She didn't have time to pull the black drape out of the bag; everything was moving too fast. She barely had time to set the aperture and f-stop, switch out the slides, and shoot. She needed four hands.

She had no doubt which man was Miles McDow. Tall and swarthy, he was full of arrogance and pride, even when handcuffed. "I'm a reporter from the *New York American*," she said, running alongside the entourage. "Do you have a statement for the press?"

He gave her a look of surprise, then laughed. "Sure, Baby. Take this down. Meet me down here day after tomorrow, and I'll take you back to Nassau with me and show you a swinging time."

Even the Coast Guard officers laughed at that remark. Clarette's face burned, but she refused to give up. "Did you know your accomplice was picked up in North Carolina yesterday?"

His expression clouded. "You're crazy. I'm up here on a pleasure cruise. I have no associate."

"Do you sell whiskey brought up from Nassau, off your ship outside the government-set boundaries?"

"You're dreaming, lady. You been reading too many dime novels. Go home and wash the dishes."

"Officer," she said, deciding to change her tack, "did they offer any resistance? Was there a struggle?"

The spit-and-polish young officer gave her a look of disdain. "Does it look like they struggled? My uniform's not even dirty."

How was she ever going to get a straight answer? If she'd met this officer at the Dixie Club or Delmonico's—that is, if he could have afforded an evening at either one—he'd have listened to every word she spoke. But not now, not here, not like this.

She continued to hammer away, until the crew of the *Artemis* was turned over to the police. Then she captured a few more photos of the notorious rumrunner as he was being loaded into the paddy wagon and carted off.

"What'd you get?" Hank asked when they were in the cab, returning to the office.

"Bits and pieces. Evidently it was a surprise. There seemed to be no resistance. I surprised him by mentioning his associate in North Carolina. He probably had no idea how he'd been found out. It'll be a great story."

Hank shook his head. "Don't bother."

She turned to him. "What's that supposed to mean?"

"There's a technicality. The police officer in charge told me. Said he wished it could be different, but they'll be back out on that ship almost before their fingerprints are dry."

Clarette felt the air go out of her. So that's why McDow had said what he had about meeting her day after tomorrow. That explained his smug attitude. He probably already knew he had a way out.

"No sense you having egg on your face. I'll take care of it. Just a little bottom corner, second page with a couple photos."

She nodded. No scoop. No front page sensational story with her name. Maybe next time. Hank gave her a fatherly pat on the shoulder. "You did a good job, though, kid. Keep hold of that contact of yours."

Back at the newsroom, she let Hank take it, and she finished the article for the society page.

## two

Clarette's third-story walk-up in the Flatbush section of Brooklyn was in sharp contrast to her family's sprawling estate in Hamptonwood, New Jersey. For that matter, it was in even sharper contrast to her Grandmother Vanderpool's brownstone on Fifth Avenue—and Grandmother Fortier's elegant mansion in Queens, where her Uncle Cavet and his family now resided.

The eight-block walk from the subway to her apartment was an invigorating challenge for her, even in winter. Somehow it fueled a deep need within her to be completely on her own. Today in the lingering warmth of the spring day, she felt especially refreshed. The walk gave her time to clear her mind of the confusion of the day.

Her mother, if she knew, would be appalled by the fact that her daughter walked to her apartment, yet her mother thought nothing of walking for hours on the links when she played golf. Those piddling inconsistencies were what infuriated Clarette about her family and her upbringing. She had no patience with such paltry thinking.

When she was in her teen years, she had needed great courage to go against her family's wishes. They were shocked when she had whizzed through boring Miss Damerow's Preparatory High School in three short years. And she would never forget the uproar when she asked to depart from the quiet campus of her high school's sister college. The teachers there were hopelessly old fashioned, their minds stuck back in the nineties. But Miss Damerow's was the only women's college in the area of which her parents approved.

By her junior year, she could stand the stifling atmosphere of the staid school no longer. In the face of her parents' protests, she transferred to Barnard's Women's College at Columbia University. Here the progressive freethinkers could be heard and learned from. She was in ecstacy.

That was when she chose to drop the Vanderpool name and take up Fortier. The Fortier name was quietly known in New York circles, but Vanderpool silks and garments were blatantly famous nationwide. She wanted to make her own way in life, not ride on her family's already established reputation.

Once she realized that her family opposed *everything* she wanted to do, no matter what it was, her life became somewhat easier. Since nothing pleased them, she decided she might as well do anything she wanted. She sought employment to pay for the final year of her education—although her Grandmother Vanderpool did secretly pay some toward her lodging and incidentals. Clarette bewildered her straitlaced Dutch grandmother, but the aging matriarch seemed to possess a measure of tolerance missing in the other members of the family.

When graduation day at Columbia rolled around, only her older brother Aubert Grandmother Vanderpool attended. But Clarette didn't care. She had scored high in all her exams, and she was proud of herself, even if her family wasn't.

As she strolled by the smaller one-family dwellings on the way to her apartment house, children squealed and played in the last rays of the spring dusk, happy that summer vacation time was near. Window boxes spilled over with pink geraniums; greening flower beds sent out rainbows of lupines and canterbury bells. Clarette breathed deeply of the aromas of flowers and supper meals being prepared throughout the neighborhood.

After mentally sorting through the day's events, she concluded she had gained more than she had lost. After all, Sid had trusted her with the assignment. That in itself was a giant leap forward. Sending Hank along was probably just an afterthought on Sid's part. But the best part of all was learning of Shanks' potential. The boy knew to keep his ears and eyes open, and he seemed eager to help. Even though this incident hadn't been fruitful, it wouldn't be her last opportunity.

In her shopping bag were two nice carp picked up at the fish market for their supper. Her roommate Herta Erhardt, a second-generation German girl, would be grateful to come home to a ready meal. While Clarette had done fairly well at teaching herself to cook, she never could catch the concept of cleaning, something to which girls from her background were never exposed, so she cooked and Herta scrubbed. After a year, they had settled into a comfortable routine.

Turning the lock in the apartment door, Clarette was met with a face full of musty air. The morning had been too chilly to throw open the windows, but she did so now before quickly changing out of the dull gray suit.

By the time Herta came in from her job at one of the garment factories on the Lower East Side, Clarette had dinner ready. The only item Clarette had not prepared was the loaf of dark bread which Herta baked every Saturday.

"I could smell supper on the first landing," Herta laughed as she kicked off her shoes by the door. "Even above Mrs. Goldberg's cabbage." Herta, who had grown up in the shadow of the Old Country, still wore dark stockings and square-heeled shoes, saying that sheer stockings were a disgrace for decent women.

"Wash up quick," Clarette told her. "It's ready."

Thankfully, Herta didn't work in one of the Vanderpool garment factories. If she had, their relationship would have become even more awkward than it had for a short time after Herta had found out Clarette's true identity. The secret had leaked when Herta had taken a phone call and Grandmother Vanderpool had asked for Clarette Vanderpool, unwittingly destroying her granddaughter's disguise.

"You could have all that luxury and high brow living—and you want to be here?" Herta had waved her muscled arm to take in the plain apartment. "That's lunacy. Sheer lunacy." After that Herta was openly resentful of the things Clarette paid for, saying they might have come from Clarette's rich family—and Herta did not wish to be beholden for any charity. Through the months, though, Clarette strove to help Herta forget about the Vanderpool money, and she thought that now Herta had nearly forgotten that Clarette's background was any different from her own.

Over dinner they exchanged news of their day. Herta daily proclaimed that nothing exciting ever happened at the garment factory, and yet she was filled with stories of the people with whom she worked. Clarette was fascinated by her stories.

"I almost made it to the front page today," Clarette said when her turn to talk came. She stood up and began clearing away the dishes.

Herta stopped pouring the cups of black coffee. "Almost? Why almost? And why are you just now telling me this exciting news?"

The comment warmed Clarette; this was *exciting news* to her roommate, even though the same bit of news would mean little to her own parents. "I almost forgot, I was so interested in your story about Nellie flirting with the foreman."

Herta pushed a mug toward Clarette. "You didn't forget."

"I didn't," Clarette admitted. "You're right. But I'm ready to tell it now."

Herta place the coffeepot back on the two-burner stove and sat her square frame back at the table. "So tell."

Briefly Clarette explained about the tip from Shanks and all that had happened after. Herta noisily slurped her coffee and nodded as she listened. When Clarette came to the part about what Hank had said about the technicality, Herta lowered her cup. "Say that again. The police told him there was a technicality?"

"I guess there wasn't enough evidence."

"But that's not what he said."

"No, he just said there was a technicality."

"Mmm." Herta slurped more coffee.

"What's the matter?"

Herta shrugged. "What did you do then?"

"I didn't do anything. Hank said there was no story, so I went to the office and finished my column."

Herta leaned forward. "Did you ever see a bird snare?"

Clarette shook her head.

"My brothers used to set them on the roof of the building where we lived on Second Street. A little rope, a little meal, a little trap. They got pretty good at snaring unsuspecting birds. Of course my brothers were good boys, and they let them go again."

"Herta, don't talk in riddles. What are you saying?"

"I may be wrong—but I think little boy Hank snared little bird Clarette."

"How?"

"You've been too protected. You're so gullible. First of all, how would an officer know there was any technicality, whether it meant a search warrant being bad or lack of evidence? And secondly, even if he did know, why would he unload that kind of information to the press? The police are usually more tight-lipped than that. Sounds to me like Hank Maxwell wanted your story."

Clarette choked and coughed as the stout coffee went down her throat the wrong way. Herta jumped up and pounded her on the back with a strong arm.

"Cut it out," Clarette managed to sputter. "I'd rather choke to death than be beat into unconsciousness." Once she caught her breath, she sat back with a sigh, overcome with disgust at her own gullibility. "How could you see it so clearly?" she wanted to know. "So quickly?"

Herta smiled. "People from the streets think alike maybe. I don't know. We have to fight for every inch, while you were showered with luxury. But that may be only part of why Hank acted the way he did."

"I think I can guess the other part," Clarette said with a sniff. "Hank didn't want to be bested by a dame. Right?"

"You said it, I didn't."

"If what you're saying is true, I deserve to lose my story. But sure as I live, it'll never happen to me again."

Herta shook her finger. "Mm-mm. Beware of saying never."

The jangling of the phone in the living room interrupted their conversation. "I hate that foolish noisy thing," Herta said as she took her cup to the sink. "The calls are always for you anyway."

Clarette ignored her friend's grumbling and picked up the phone. She was surprised to hear her mother's voice on the other end. Seldom did Mother call, unless it was an emergency. But as Clarette listened, she realized this was no emergency.

"This is your father's fiftieth birthday, darling." Her mother's voice was clipped and brief, the way it always was now whenever she spoke with her daughter. "He wants you to come and be a part of the festivities on Saturday. Perhaps you could take the train up here Friday evening rather than going back to. . ." She hesitated, Clarette knew, because Viletta Vanderpool could not fathom this little apartment being the home of her daughter. "Going back to your place," she continued at last. "Then you could stay over until Sunday."

Clarette hadn't forgotten her father's birthday. She had planned to sneak up to his office on Friday and give him his gift. But now that she had been invited home—an invitation that had not been extended of late—she felt she'd better accept.

"Thank you, Mother. I'll be there."

She could hear her mother's sigh. Obviously, she had thought Clarette would refuse to come—and then, Clarette thought cynically, how would she have explained her daughter's absence to her friends and family? Appearances were of utmost importance to Mother.

"Thank you, my dear," her mother said. "Your father will be so appreciative. I'll have Aubert meet you at the station."

*Wonderful*, Clarette thought. That would give her older brother at least thirty minutes to lecture her before they reached the house. For a moment she regretted her undercover act; if not for her disguise, she could have simply ridden home with her father in his touring car. She sighed. "Tell Aubert I'll be watching for him. I'll see you Friday evening."

Clarette wanted to let Herta know how much she appreciated her insight and wisdom; but now that her roommate had overheard the conversation between Clarette and her mother, the stark difference in their backgrounds would once more be at the front of Herta's mind. Clarette resented the fact that her family had the power to do that. And she was distressed that it obviously bothered Herta so much.

"I can barely imagine what your own bedroom must look like," Herta had said once, "let alone the whole house. Your room alone is probably bigger than our entire apartment."

The problem was, Herta was right. Her bedroom at the house in Hamptonwood was spacious, sunny, and had a private dressing room overflowing with silk robes and gowns. Beyond that was her private bath, stocked with shelves full of fluffy soft towels. But strangely enough, Clarette never missed any of it.

After the dishes were washed and dried, the two young women sat together in the small living room. Spring warmth came in the open window, along with the muffled sounds of traffic and the barking of a stray dog.

Herta busily darned a pair of stockings. Clarette's grandmother did exquisite hand work, but before she had come to live with Herta she had never seen anyone darn stockings. The ease with which Herta's long needle flew in and out fascinated Clarette. She opened a new novel she was reading, but her eyes kept wandering back to that flashing needle.

"I'll be gone this weekend," she said.

"I heard."

"I'll be back Sunday afternoon, though. Want to go to Coney Island Sunday night?"

"I better go to church. Besides, I'm trying to save my money."

Clarette opened her mouth to say she would pay, but she thought better of it. "You've been going to church a lot lately, haven't you?"

Herta looked up. "It's good to go to church. And it wouldn't hurt you to go either, you know."

"I go to church," Clarette protested, "when I feel like it." When Herta didn't answer, she added, "I haven't seen much to impress me in the churches I've attended."

Herta sniffed. "Political churches."

"Political?"

"All they talk about is Prohibition, or how they got President Harding elected, or what's going on in Tammany Hall."

"What do they talk about at your church, Herta?" Clarette put her open book upside down in her lap.

"The Lord, of course. How to serve Him."

"Maybe I'll come and visit your church sometime." Clarette was mildly curious. She wasn't particularly interested in talking about the Lord, but she would like to know her roommate better. Grandmother Vanderpool now and then talked to Clarette about her need for salvation, though, and that, Clarette thought, was a bore, something she definitely did not want more of in her life.

"You could visit my church," Herta was saying now, her voice expressionless, "if you had a mind to. I'm not sure how you'd be accepted. Your background might make people uncomfortable."

"Just introduce me as your friend. No one has to know more than that." Clarette paused. "I am your friend, aren't I?"

Herta's needle continued to fly. "I hadn't thought much about it. I suppose so."

Clarette put her silver book marker in her book. "I'm going to leave the phone number of our place in Hamptonwood on the table here. If I have any calls from the office, would you call me there?"

Herta looked up. "Long distance?"

Clarette tried not to smile. She wondered what Herta would think if she told her that her father talked to people in Europe, London, even Mexico by phone every day. "It's probably just wishful thinking on my part," she said, "but maybe I'll get an assignment—and I don't want to miss it. Will you call? I'll pay for it."

Herta went back to her darning. "I suppose a maid will answer," she said curtly, as though having a maid were a sin.

"She might." Clarette stood and stretched. "Or Mother might pick it up herself—if she's in an energetic mood." She looked at Herta and saw that the humor was wasted on her; she was too intent on making her stockings last through another season.

"Herta," Clarette said as she went to the bedroom door, "I want to thank you for the wisdom you shared with me at supper. You helped give me a greater understanding of what I'm up against."

Herta's eyes never left her stocking. "Sounds like you're going to need all the understanding you can get."

No-nonsense Herta. Clarette wondered if the girl ever had any fun at all.

❧

The next morning when Clarette stepped from the subway kiosk, she found out that Herta had been right. The newsboys were shouting, "Extra! Extra! Git yer paper here. Rumrunner McDow charged with bootlegging from aboard schooner *Artemis*. Read all about it!" Hank had stolen Clarette's story.

# three

Clarette dropped a coin in the grubby hand of a newsboy and grabbed a copy of the *American*. And there it was, emblazoned on the front page with Maxwell's byline. *The gall of the man.* But then, he hadn't exactly had to fight her for it.

The crush of people surged about her as she scanned the first few paragraphs. McDow had been fingerprinted and booked. Hank Maxwell had unabashedly lied to her, just as Herta had predicted.

She tried to imagine her shock if Herta had not prepared her for this. Hank Maxwell was probably up in the newsroom this very moment, laughing himself silly with the other men. Shame and anger stirred inside her. Hank was so certain she'd never make it as a reporter, and he never failed to tell her so. She should have known better than to be so easily duped.

She folded the newspaper, tucked it under her arm, and hurried down Sixth, toward Bryant Park near the library for her meeting with Shanks. He was snapping his rag for a dapper man in a flat-brimmed straw hat as she approached. She sat down on a park bench in the sunshine to watch him create a sheen on the man's expensive shoes. When he finished, she called to him. His eyes lit up as he hurried toward her, the box banging his side as he loped along.

"Mornin', Miss Clarie." He pulled off the battered hat and set the box on the grass.

"Good morning, Shanks." She unfolded the newspaper to show him. "Your tip was right on the money."

He smiled. "Ain't no surprise to me. I done heard 'em talking about it." The smile turned to a scowl as he leaned toward the

24

paper. Even though Shanks wasn't in school very often, Clarette knew he was learning to read. "That ain't your name there. Somebody swipe your story?"

"Sort of. Here's your money, though. Go buy your breakfast. And be sure it goes to breakfast, just like we agreed."

The boy shoved his hands into the deep pockets of the oversized pants. "I ain't taking no money since it ain't your story no more."

Clarette was touched. "Hey, that's silly. That part was entirely my fault, not yours, and you can bet it won't happen again. I'm paying you for a great tip. You deserve every cent of it." She leaned over and dropped the coins into his shoe shine box. "Now get on your way. I'm late for work."

"Much obliged, Miss Clarie." He lifted the clumsy box and hefted the strap over his shoulder. "Sorry you lost the story, but I's going to keep my ears open for more good tips."

"You do that," she called after him, "and don't forget to eat breakfast." He waved his long arm without looking back.

Just as she had expected, the men in the newsroom were twittering like magpies as she walked in. In spite of the sinking feeling deep inside her, she lifted her head, set her chin, and braced herself.

"Great lead story, Maxwell," someone called out.

"Man oh man, does Hank have a nose for news," came another taunt followed by snickers and laughter.

"I don't know how you do it," said another. "What an exclusive. Not even the *Times* did as well."

"When you got it, you got it," she heard Hank reply as she sat down at her typewriter.

She could have made a number of remarks, but for now she held her silence. In her opinion, Hank Maxwell was a thief and a liar, but it was her word against his. She had no way of knowing what he'd told his cronies about the previous day's events, but obviously his account had been at her expense. If she tried to tell her side, it would only be her word against his.

Later in the morning, Hank strolled by her desk. "Got any more leads I can help you with, Miss Fortier?"

He wasn't satisfied with just taking her story, he was bent on rubbing it in. Her disgust was mounting. "I used to think I wouldn't like having a woman hanging around here," he went on, "but I've changed my mind. Now I think it's gonna be great fun. Great fun." He gave a horse-laugh in appreciation of his own joke.

"Glad I could be of service to you, Mr. Maxwell," she replied softly. "Too bad you aren't enough of a newsman to find your own leads. Have to take them from a woman."

Hank's voice went hard and low. "Why should I knock myself out when there's a dumb female fall-guy so ready and willing?"

Clarette pulled her copy from her typewriter and stood up. "Whatever did you do for leads before this dumb female fall-guy came along to rescue you?" she asked sweetly, then pushed by him to go show her copy to the Chief.

Having the last word gave her only a moment of satisfaction. He'd proven what a man's world she was in, but she was confident things were changing. She would chalk this experience up as a valuable lesson, one that she wouldn't need to repeat twice.

❧

That evening she caught the train at Grand Central for Hamptonwood. As she watched the tall buildings of her home city rush past the windows, she wished once again that she hadn't let the McDow story slip from her grasp so easily. The timing would have been perfect; she could have put the paper, with her name on the front page, into her father's hands for his birthday. She could have proven to him that she really was making a difference in the world.

Her father enjoyed fine literature and had a library to prove it, but he had a low opinion of the newfangled syndicated newspapers and those who wrote for them. "Journalists used to wield power," he told her once. "Now the syndicates rule and reign. It's just another big business."

Her decision to become a reporter was just one more item on the list of how Clarette had displeased and disappointed her family.

The station at Hamptonwood was bustling with commuters. The New Jersey community, Clarette mused, was becoming a mere suburb of teeming New York City. She could see her brother's tall, slender form waiting for her on the platform. His pale yellow suit with the matching silk shirt and soft gray spats gave him the poised, finished look of the rich. Every dark hair was meticulously in place. His pinched face, however, was as serious as ever. Aubert was trapped in the sober business of keeping up appearances, a pastime that interested Clarette not at all.

"Aubert! Over here!" Her call brought his head around. Twittering society females swooned over his face, Clarette knew, but she thought his nose a trifle long, his lips rather thin. His long legs brought him quickly to her side.

She hadn't expected a warm welcome from him, and she wasn't disappointed when all he said was, "Is this all you brought?" He pointed at her small bag.

"Hello, Aubert. You're looking good. Nice to see you again." She waved her hand at his shirt and grinned. "I hear silks are all the rage this year. Smart choice." But he had not time or patience for her sarcasm.

"Come, prodigal child. Your parents are waiting."

She could see this was going to be a long weekend.

She fell in behind his long strides to where his roadster was parked. "Let me drive," she begged, following him around to the driver's side. She loved the feel of being in command of such a powerful machine, and she hadn't had a chance to drive for a number of months.

Aubert pondered her request. "Please?" she pleaded. She felt a little the way she had when as a child she had wanted to play with his electric railroad set. She had played with it much more often than he had, but she had still had to beg for permission each time she had taken it out of its crate.

"Oh, I suppose." Aubert tossed her the key and threw her things in the back seat. "Perhaps it will diffuse your excess energy so that you'll be calm by dinner time."

The stretch of graded road lay invitingly before her. The air here among the trees blew cooler than in the city. She breathed in the clean scents of spring. What fun it would be to drive and drive, on and on in an endless adventure of seeking out new places and doing new things. Her spirit hungered inside of her, reaching out toward some unknown thing that lay over the horizon.

In the metro area, the speed limit was ten miles an hour, but once she was out in the country she took the roadster to well above thirty, even on the winding curves. Twice her brother warned her to slow down. "You'll smash us into a tree, you silly girl."

"Oh, you're too stuffy, Aubert." She pulled off her cloche hat and tossed it into the seat behind her, letting the wind ruffle her bob. "Don't you ever have any fun?"

"I can have fun without taking senseless risks."

"Can you?"

"Of course I can."

"In my opinion, it's taking risks that makes life fun."

Aubert stretched out his long legs and relaxed as she slowed the speed back down to twenty. "You wouldn't talk silly like this if you'd stayed where you belonged at Miss Damerow's."

"What makes you think I wouldn't?" She'd not heard this opinion from her brother before.

He looked over at her with his serious eyes that had forgotten how to laugh. When they had been in grammar school, people had said they looked enough alike to be twins. She could still see the resemblance when she looked at their portraits in the family album: the same narrow jaw and dark eyes they had gotten from Grandmother Fortier, the same long, barely turned-up nose from their mother. But now as she looked at him she could recognize nothing of herself in his face.

"Miss Damerow's is a fine school," he told her, "where you would have learned decorum and discretion, not women's rights and Sigmund Freud."

"No matter where I studied, I'd still be me."

"Perhaps. But you'd be a better you."

"I'd be as boring as all my staid ancestors."

"Our ancestors are all people to be proud of—people to emulate."

"Really? Then why aren't you sailing to China on a clipper ship, bringing back yards of silk, rather than sitting in an office making boring deals on the telephone and—"

"Not that way!" Aubert interrupted her. He reached over and pulled on the steering wheel. By instinct she had almost turned down the road to the sturdy old two-story where the two of them had grown up.

"Okay, I got it." She smacked at his interfering hand. Her parents were now at the impressive Vanderpool Estate a few more miles down the road.

Their life in the old house had existed when the Vanderpool business had been in silks and silks alone. Since then, the business had mushroomed into several garment factories, a new boutique on Fifth Avenue, and now, the newest twist, her father's interest in the stock exchange.

"Back to my question. . ." Clarette prodded.

"The ability to sail a clipper ship wasn't the quality I was recommending that you emulate, Clarette, and you know it."

She turned the smooth-running roadster into the long wooded drive leading up to the mansion that her parents now called home.

The grandiose, buff-stucco building with red-tiled roof was a replica of an Italian villa her mother had seen a few years previously on a visit to the Mediterranean. How glad Clarette was that she did not live here.

"I tell you what, brother dear. You choose who you want to emulate, and I'll choose who I want to emulate—and we'll get along perfectly." She pulled the car to a stop near the tiered marble fountain that graced the entrance.

"You're impossible." Aubert jumped out and grabbed her bag. "Just see to it you don't let your wild, erratic ideas spoil Daddy's birthday."

Clarette reached in the back seat for her hat. She came up behind her brother as he stalked across the gravel drive, and standing on tiptoe, she pulled her cloche hat down over his head, mussing his impeccable hair. Her giggles filled the prim air around the mansion.

Dropping the bag, Aubert pulled off her hat and stood looking at her for a moment. "Your games are not amusing, Clarette. This is exactly the kind of thing I was referring to a moment ago." With no emotion, he smoothed back his hair and handed her the hat.

Something deep inside her longed to crack his veneer; surely somewhere inside him was the little boy she had played with. She sighed and followed him up the sweeping marble steps.

She recognized few of the household staff. In the years since she'd been away at school many servants had left, replaced by new people. Aubert gave her bag to a lofty-looking butler and ordered him to see that it was taken to Clarette's room. "Mother will be waiting for you in her sitting room," Aubert said to Clarette. "I suggest you see her now."

"I can see her at dinner. I'd like to change first and get out of this garb." She was still dressed in her gray suit, and she felt hot and stifled, anxious to trade her clothes for something filmy and light. Besides, she knew her mother would prefer to see her attired in something other than the plain, business-like suit.

"She's waiting for you," Aubert said as Clarette followed him up the winding white staircase and around the balcony above.

"When will Daddy be home?"

"Another hour or so."

"Then I'll see them both at dinner."

Aubert stood still and looked at her. "You live as though your family doesn't exist, you won't carry the name you were born with, you stay away for months, and now that you're here, you don't even have the decency to go greet your own mother."

"Oh, all right. Don't get yourself worked into a lather." Clarette realized she might as well go along with what her brother wanted; after all, she'd soon be out of here, back to the freedom of her own life.

Her mother's sitting room was located off the master suite on the second floor. The spacious room was done in bold, floral chintz. Clarette recognized many of her mother's favorite French paintings, displayed on the walls in lavish gold frames. Two of her mother's most famous hats were on shiny brass stands; they dated from the days when Viletta Fortier had been one of the more well known names in New York millinery. That had been before the handsome silk dealer, Johannes Vanderpool, had come to snatch her out of her work-a-day world.

Clarette always wondered if her mother missed it. Missed the challenge and creativity, the feeling of independence. Even though Viletta was forever involved in charitable and political causes, could they provide the same stimulus?

Her mother, who hated dreary winter days, had chosen the south part of the house for maximum sunshine. Clarette looked about the empty room, then saw the open french doors which led to a veranda. She strode softly across the deep oriental rug and stepped out into the early evening sunshine.

Viletta was seated primly in a white wicker chair, reading a book and sipping an iced drink. Small glass-topped wrought-iron tables were scattered about among the sturdy wicker furniture. Cushions and pillows echoed the bright floral prints from the sitting room.

At the sound of the door, Viletta lowered her book and looked up. "So you did come."

Clarette nodded. "I just came in to say hello. I need to change."

Her mother surveyed the gray suit and cloche hat. "I definitely agree that you should change. What a ghastly combination."

Clarette knew her mother hated the newest styles in hats. "Little bits of ugly nothing," she had said when the cloche had first appeared in the marketplace. Clarette was also certain her mother did not approve of her bob.

"The suit may be ugly, but it's good for work." Clarette closed the distance between them and leaned to give her mother a kiss on the cheek.

"When I had my millinery shop, I wore lovely gowns," her mother said, apparently oblivious to the kiss. "I was a businesswoman, but I saw no need to look like a man."

"Times have changed."

"So they say. Dinner will be served at seven-thirty in the Green Room. Your Grandmother Vanderpool is here."

Clarette brightened. In spite of her grandmother's tendency to talk too much about God and the Bible, Clarette appreciated her warmth. "And the party tomorrow?"

"A luncheon will be served on the lawn east of the pool and bathhouse. I've kept it small, only about fifty guests. The invitations said half past noon."

Clarette nodded and turned to go. "I'll see you at dinner."

"Clarette?"

"Yes, Mother?"

"It's good for your father that you agreed to come."

*Good for Daddy? Now what in the world did that mean?*

# four

Dinner that evening was a stiff, quiet affair. Other than a warm hug from Grandmother Vanderpool, plus her smiles and winks through dinner, the whole evening was stuffy and dull. Clarette would have preferred to dance the night away at a jazz club in Harlem. Father sat at the head of the table wearing his tweeds, his pince-nez, and his gleaming watch fob, exactly as she remembered him from her childhood. His dark hair showed a smidgen of gray at the temples, but his erect figure was as trim as ever.

The soup had barely been served before conversation turned to if and when Clarette would be coming home to stay. "One would think," her mother said in a pained tone, "that by now I would have grandchildren. All your school chums from Miss Damerow's are settled down with husbands and children. And here you are living like . . . Like I don't know what."

Clarette could just imagine the kind of man her mother would choose for her to marry. One with clean, manicured nails and slicked back hair. A man who sat comfortably in the lap of his father's booming business. Although she herself wasn't altogether certain what kind of man she wished to marry, she knew a good manicure was not one of her criteria.

"Aubert's the firstborn," she protested. "Let him produce grandchildren. How about it, Aubert? Anyone special you've been courting?" She was trying desperately to avert the discussion from herself.

"I'm probably in a better position to be married than you might think," her brother said in his usual matter-of-fact manner.

"See, Mother? There you are. I'm sure it won't be any time at all before you will be a grandmother."

"That's not what I meant, Clarette, and you know it," her mother retorted. "You should be here in your home. You should be making your place in the family."

Clarette took a deep breath. "Might I remind you it was you who sent me off to Miss Damerow's when I was barely thirteen?"

"Of course we did. That was to train you to fulfill your rightful position. But you've chosen to turn your back on your own heritage."

Clarette was beginning to wish she'd never come. Her father's birthday wasn't worth listening to all this.

"Newspapers today are nothing like they used to be," her father stated midway through the second course. He broached the subject as though continuing an ongoing discussion.

"In what way, Father?" Aubert asked politely.

"Independent thinking has fallen by the wayside. All journalism has lost its flair and flavor." Daddy firmed the glasses on his nose.

Grandmother Vanderpool winked at Clarette. "That's rather an unfair generalization, don't you think?" she asked her son.

"Not at all, Mother, not at all. I tell you the mass consolidation has resulted in canned thoughts and canned thinking. There used to be opposing opinions in the various papers. Now they buy ideas like they buy train cars full of bulk newsprint. It's a disgrace and an insult to independent thinkers like myself."

This tirade was obviously for Clarette's benefit. She was being told in a roundabout fashion that her father approved of her no more than her mother did. She did not try to defend herself, but quietly continued to eat, hoping that eventually the conversation would turn to something else.

After supper, her father and brother retired to the smoking room where their cigars smoke would turn the room blue as they discussed upcoming business deals. Mother returned to her sitting room where, she said with a sigh, she had mounds of letters to be answered.

Grandmother Vanderpool invited Clarette to come out to the veranda with her. The night was cool, with a clear warm sky lit by a hazy half moon. Scents of springtime hung in the air. A slight breeze ruffled Clarette's short hair and whipped at her gauzy skirt.

Grandmother seated herself in a cushioned chaise. From hardy Dutch stock, the woman seemed as strong and sturdy as she'd been ten years earlier, unlike fragile Grandmother Fortier who had recently fallen ill and died.

As Clarette settled in the nearby glider, she felt her grandmother studying her. After a moment, Grandmother said, "I believe you're one of the few young ladies who can wear bobbed hair and still remain attractive."

Clarette thought about the remark. "Thank you," she said after a moment.

"It's so daring. I admire your courage, Clarette."

Compliments were rare in her family. Two in a row were almost unheard of, so Clarette simply nodded and smiled. Cutting her long hair a year ago hadn't been nearly as difficult as several of the other stands she had taken to preserve her individuality.

"Are you happy, Clarette? Happy with where you are and what you are doing?"

Clarette thought a moment. "Happier than I've ever been."

"That's good to hear." They fell silent as the orchestra of insect symphonies tuned up across the vast lawn and throughout the woods and gardens. Croaking frogs from the fish pond joined in the chorus. Presently Grandmother spoke again. "Although your mother and father may not understand just now, I feel someday they will."

"It doesn't matter. I've given up hoping for their understanding."

"The Lord is going to use you, Clarette."

Clarette choked back a chuckle. "Me? I rather doubt it."

But Grandmother acted as though she hadn't heard. "You remind me of Saul of Tarsus pushing headlong on your own mission. Doing what you think is right, and doing it with all your might. But there'll come a time, just as there did for Saul, when the Lord will stop you and speak to you."

This was an interesting concept Clarette had not heard before. She looked over at her grandmother. The moonlight gleamed on her silvery hair, and the old woman was staring off into the night, almost as though she could see the reality of what she was saying. Clarette shivered.

"And when He does," Grandmother went on, "I want you to remember a scripture, my dear. It's found in the sixteenth chapter of Proverbs, verse nine. 'A man's heart deviseth his way: but the Lord directeth his steps.'"

Grandmother Vanderpool stopped a moment and adjusted the pillow behind her back. "You just think you're heading in a certain direction. But I pray for you daily, and I believe it is the Lord who is directing your steps. You may be quite surprised where those steps will lead."

Part of Clarette wanted to ask her grandmother to explain—and another part wanted the old woman to hush. She could deal with her family's indifference, she realized, easier than she could the confusing sensation that her grandmother's words gave her.

"Well, I hope the Lord knows enough to let my steps lead right into the Chief's office with a great story," she said lightly. She stood and feigned a wide yawn. "Guess I'd better get to bed. I'm more tired than I'd thought."

She turned to go, but her grandmother held out her hands. Clarette had no choice but to lean over and take them. The old woman drew her gently down and placed a soft kiss on her cheek. "Good night, my dear. Sleep well. God loves you."

Clarette was an expert at making herself hard in the face of her parents' and Aubert's disapproval, but she was not prepared for this kind of affection. She felt a sudden pain in her heart. "Thank you, Grandmother Vanderpool," she whispered. She strained to collect her poise. "I'll probably skip breakfast, so I'll see you at Daddy's party."

In her room, Clarette changed into her silk nightgown and scrubbed her face at the marble lavatory with its gold-plated spigots, drying with the plush towels that matched the walls with their shades of rose. Strange, she mused, that this was considered her suite when she was so seldom here.

She stepped up the cherry wood steps to the massive canopied feather bed. How easy it could be to allow all this luxury to suck her into its grasp, like sinking into the featherbed's soft comfort. *Soft*. That was the word that described Aubert and his life. She never wanted to be like her brother, drifting along on the coattails of the family business.

She bounded back up out of the bed, strode to the bay windows, and pulled open the drapes. The moon was higher now, not so fat, and no longer golden, but a chalky white. She fluffed the pillows in the window seat and settled herself among them. She was certain what she *didn't* want in life—but what *did* she want?

She hadn't meant to fall asleep, but she awoke after midnight with a crick in her neck. Sleepily, she rose from the window seat and yielded to the featherbed's soft cradle.

ક

The next morning when she looked out her window, past the terraced gardens toward the bath house, workers were already setting up a grand array of pastel tents on the rolling lawn. Inside the tents, she knew, would be food tables, an orchestra, and seating for the guests.

When she went into the adjoining dressing room, she found that someone—probably her mother—had laid out a summer dress the color of a robin's egg. The strapped pumps and broad-brimmed straw hat, decked with soft flowers, were a perfect match. Her mother had never lost her flair for elegant style and class, Clarette had to admit that. Clarette hadn't even thought about what she would wear today, but she resented having the decision made for her. If it hadn't been her father's birthday, she would have refused.

She waited until nearly one before she slowly strolled out through the veranda and down the shady stone steps of the terraced gardens. Fountains beside the veranda wall echoed the larger one at the mansion entrance. The water spilled and splashed from the lower fountains down a series of miniature waterfalls, cutting through well-tended plats of shrubs and flowers, until it reached the bottom fish pond where it circled lazily beneath the blooming water lilies.

Clarette made her way past the summer house out onto the back lawn where sprawling shade trees and the pastel tents offered respite from the midday sunshine. As Clarette walked among the guests, she felt the stares as heads turned. Her mother came up beside her and said softly, "Now you look like a Vanderpool."

Clarette grimaced. "That's what I was afraid of."

Her mother sucked in a breath. "I don't understand you, Clarette."

"And you probably never will," her daughter answered softly before she moved on.

She saw no one she particularly cared to speak to. Most of the guests were older couples the age of her parents. No young people like the crowd she partied with in the city. Still, the day was perfect with bright skies and just a touch of breeze. Lilting chamber music drifted from the direction of the orchestra tent. The chef and his workers had created masterpieces with the food tables. Food sculptures gave an appearance of an array of plants and flowers rather than mere lowly food.

She had already given her father his gift after dinner the night before, not that it had been much: a pair of mother-of-pearl cufflinks. What does one give a man who has everything—and what he doesn't have, he can buy for himself?

As she strolled near a group of men, she overheard their discussion on whether or not rayon would take over the silk industry. "Before it ever does, I'll diversify," she heard her father say. "I'm ready to change with the times and stay in the forefront of the garment industry."

Clarette marveled at the comment. She wondered if her father really could change with the times. He seemed to her so hopelessly mired in ancient traditions.

As she maneuvered back toward the food buffet, she heard her grandmother call her. Clarette looked toward the house and saw the matriarch coming down the steps from the veranda. Clarette hurried in that direction.

"Clarette, come to the house. Hurry. There's a long distance telephone call for you."

"Who is it?"

"Herta, I think she said. Isn't she your roommate?"

"That she is." Clarette's pace quickened. She hoped Herta had good news.

She took the call in her father's downstairs study where she could close the door. "Hello, Herta. What's cooking?"

"Clarette? Is that really you?"

Clarette smiled. Herta, she knew, was terrified of the telephone. "It's me. Really me."

"Well, at least I didn't get a maid. The woman who answered said she was your grandmother."

"Yes. You spoke to my Grandmother Vanderpool. But what is it, Herta? Why are you calling?"

"The man where you work called for you here. He wants you to call him."

"Which man, Herta? Who?"

"Sid Epstein."

"The Chief himself. Gracious. Just a minute." She quickly

pulled a pen from the holder on her father's desk and found a scrap of paper, then scribbled down the number Herta gave her. "Did he say what he wanted?"

"Just that he was in a hurry. I'm glad I was able to get you."

"Me too. Thanks for calling. I really appreciate it. See you tomorrow."

She clicked the receiver on the pedestal phone, then gave Central the number. It wasn't the number for *American's* office, so perhaps it was Sid's home. His voice came on the line, sounding loud and cheerful.

"Ah, Miss Fortier. Glad we could get hold of you. Got a real winner of an assignment for you."

Her heart slipped into a faster gear. "Just me—or with Mr. Maxwell?"

"This one's all yours, sweetheart. There's been an uprising of the colored people in Tulsa, Oklahoma. I want you to go to Tulsa and cover the story."

# five

Clarette could hardly believe what she was hearing. Tulsa was halfway across the continent. "You mean an Indian uprising, don't you? Don't they have Indians out there?"

"I guarantee you, it ain't the Indians. From what I hear, it's been like a war out there. But I gotta know first hand."

*What a wretched place to have to go, out in the middle of nowhere.* She felt as though she were being sent away, banished.

"Well, what do you say? Maxwell seemed to think you'd be able to handle it. He's the one who suggested you go. You've wanted your own story. Now's your chance. Will you take it or do I send one of the fellas?"

So that was it. She should have known Hank would use any opportunity to get her out of his way. If that was his little game, then she'd gladly play along. "Sure, Sid, I'll take it. Be glad to take it." She'd find the story behind the story and show them all.

"I need you to leave town pronto. Where are you and how quick can you leave?"

"I'm in Jersey. I'll catch the next train back to Brooklyn, pack this evening, and leave early in the morning."

"That should do. Let me know which train you're taking. I'll meet you at the station, give you an expense check, and bring the camera and plenty of film."

"Right. I'll call as soon as I know." She hung up the phone and stood motionless for a moment, dazed. *All the way to Tulsa. A podunk place in the middle of nowhere.* Well, podunk or not, she'd make the best of it. This was her big chance.

41

Grandmother Vanderpool was waiting in the hall. "Is everything all right?"

"Everything is just wonderful, Grandmother." She pulled off the stylish broad-brimmed hat. "I need a favor. I've got to get back home right away. I need you to go with me to the station and bring the car back."

"Your father has two chauffeurs. I'll get one of them for you."

"I don't want to use Father's chauffeurs." She paused as she tried to stop her pounding heart. "Will you do it? Please?"

Her grandmother smiled. "If you tell me what's up."

"I'll tell you on the way. Meet me at the garage in ten minutes." She ran down the hallway toward the stairs. She'd let Grandmother explain to her parents; she didn't have time to do it herself. Besides, as Mother had admitted, they'd never understand.

Clarette changed into her suit, laid the lovely dress across the bed, and packed her bag. Hopefully with the party being held on the far side of the estate, no one would notice her leaving.

Four cars were in the garage, but she knew they'd better not touch Aubert's roadster. "Let's take the coupe," Grandmother Vanderpool said. "I used that one when Aubert taught me to drive. Now I'm certainly glad I insisted on learning." She lifted the flounces of her party dress as she climbed in the passenger seat.

As they sped down the long driveway and out on the road toward town, Clarette explained her new assignment, then added, "I've been given the opportunity to prove to them I can cover a story just as well as a man."

"I believe you can do it, dear. How long will you be gone?"

"Sid said maybe a week or so." She took her eyes from the road a moment. "Grandmother, do you really believe I can do it?"

"I've watched you for many years, my dear. You've always done what you've set your mind to. This won't be any different."

"Except that this is more important than anything I've ever

done. I can't fail."

At the station her grandmother pulled from her handbag a small, black leather-bound book. "Here," she said, pressing it into Clarette's hand. "This Bible belonged to your Grandfather Vanderpool. He never took a voyage without it. He not only charted his journeys by God's Word, but he charted his very life by it. I've carried it since the day he died."

Clarette started to protest. "I'm not going away forever—"

But Grandmother shushed her. "I've been planning to give it to you for a long time. And this seems to be the perfect moment. I've placed a red ribbon to mark the scripture in Proverbs I told you about last night."

The shrill train whistle sounded its warning, and the porter called, "All aboard!" Clarette turned to go, but her grandmother gently held her arm. "Never forget that God is the one Who guides your steps. I will be praying for you, my dear." The stocky lady embraced Clarette and kissed her cheek.

"Thank you, Grandmother, but I've got to hurry. 'Bye." She ran toward the train. "Thanks for driving the car back. Explain to Daddy for me."

"I will, my dear. I will."

Once she was settled on the train, Clarette stuffed the little book into her bag. She appreciated the gift, but she wished her grandmother would cease her endless talking about God. When she and her friends discussed God, it was in the abstract and never bothered her in the least—but something about Grandmother's references to God made Clarette uncomfortable.

❧

Herta was dumbfounded to learn that Clarette was going on such a long trip. Clarette didn't have the heart to admit she had been to Paris twice and to London several times. But going to Europe and Great Britain was certainly different than this. She wasn't even sure what to take. She had seen Will Rogers in the *Follies*, dressed in his boots, chaps, and cowboy hat, swinging a lariat. Did everyone in Oklahoma dress like a cowboy?

She threw several lightweight dresses into the suitcase. The weather was bound to be hot, she thought. She added one of her evening dresses and her knickerbockers for good measure. Then came her new portable Underwood typewriter. She fastened the nine-pound machine securely in its carrying case and placed it by the door with her bags.

&

At Penn Station the next morning, Sid handed her the train ticket and her expense check. In his usual gruff voice, he instructed her to work with the people at the *Tulsa World* if possible, warned her to be careful, and insisted she not take any unnecessary risks. "Racial unrest is stinky and ugly," he told her. "We saw it in Chicago and Omaha. You never know who's on what side. Just get the story quick as you can and get your pretty carcass back here. I ain't paying for no more nights at that hotel than I have to."

His cigar flipped from one corner of his mouth to the other as he reached inside his coat pocket. "Here's a few bits of info I could dig up on Tulsa." He handed her an envelope, then shook her hand. "See you in a week."

"Thanks, Sid. I'll do a good job."

"You'd better," he snapped. But he gave her a grin.

&

Train dining cars had always fascinated Clarette, with their crisp white linen napkins folded in pyramid fashion, their softly flowered china, and gleaming silverware and serving trays. Dusky rose damask draperies, with tassel fringes, separated the tables. The waiter, dressed in an immaculate uniform of white duck, set before her a plate of cold slices of roast veal with fruit and sauces on the side. She smiled and thanked him, but after her third day of travel, she felt bloated and travel-weary. If she saw another rich tart or cream-filled eclair, she felt she might throw up.

The further the train carried her from New York, the warmer the air became. The fan mounted on the rosewood molding above the dining car door had precious little effect. At least, though, all the iced drinks were a delight.

She had never traveled so far all alone. With no one to talk to, the time seemed to drag. Her Pullman was comfortable, the berth cozy, but she felt drained from the incessant rocking movement and the stifling heat.

She reminded herself how badly she wanted this adventure. She thought of Hank Maxwell and tried to imagine him telling the Chief to send her to Tulsa. Thinking of that made her more determined.

She spent a good part of the journey in the secluded writing desk area, where she could read, write, or study the materials about Tulsa that Sid had given her. One brochure showed photographs and told facts about the city. The notation on the back indicated it had been published by the Tulsa Commercial Club. Named there were the major oil companies which headquartered in the city.

A photo of the high school building showed it to be half a block square, with plans to expand the next year to a full block square. Nearby Kendall College had recently changed its name to Tulsa University. A university? Perhaps she'd been a bit hasty in her judgment of this place.

From what she could learn from the notes and clippings, a few lawless Negroes had started shooting into a crowd of white men and subsequently started the riot. Some burning had occurred in the Negro area of town, called Greenwood. *Probably a few shacks on the edge of Tulsa,* Clarette reasoned.

Different clippings named conflicting numbers of deaths resulting from the riot. That seemed strange. It should be easy enough, although gruesome, to count dead bodies. This was certainly not what she was accustomed to, however. During the short layover in St. Louis, she bought a newspaper and read an even different account. No wonder Sid wanted a firsthand report.

She arose from the dining car, having eaten only a small portion of the roast veal, and returned to the passenger car. The panorama passing by the windows since early morning was fascinating—rolling hills and wide open spaces. She couldn't help but stare at the miles of treeless hills, dotted with only an occasional farmhouse, or a few cattle grazing on the tall prairie grass. She had never seen anything like this. Accustomed to the dense woods of New Jersey and the dense buildings of New York, this wide open country piqued her interest and curiosity. What kind of people would live on such rugged land?

By the time the conductor announced they were a few minutes outside Tulsa, the train cars had turned into ovens. The air blowing in the partially opened windows was hot as a blast from a furnace. Clarette was thankful she had brought her short dresses, but she wished she could pull off her silk stockings and go barefoot.

From the station, she could see glimpses of the downtown, and she was surprised by the clean, new look of the cluster of tall buildings. None of the sooty, grimy look of New York City. No wonder they had dubbed Tulsa the "Magic City."

By the time the Negro porter had gathered her bags and hailed a taxi, she had broken into a sweat. "Is it always this hot here?" she asked the smiling porter.

"Oh no, ma'am," he said shaking his head. "By Fourth of July, it'll be a whole lot hotter. So hot you can fry an egg on the hood of the banker's Pierce Arrow, if'n you should take a notion." He chuckled.

She couldn't imagine weather any hotter. The air was still and thick, and her breathing felt labored.

The hotel, located at Third and Cincinnati, was only a few blocks from the train station. Several buildings were under construction, and evidence of oil boom money was everywhere. When she asked him, the cabbie pointed out the office of the *Tulsa World*. She was glad to see it was within walking distance of her hotel—that is, if she could walk in this stifling heat.

The lobby of the Hotel Tulsa was as elaborate as anything she had seen in New York, with crystal chandeliers, gold tracery on the ceilings, and elaborate murals on one wall. Whirring ceiling fans moved the warm air about the lobby among the milling crowd.

Clarette soon would learn that a crowd was always in this lobby. Many of the rooms in the hotel had become temporary offices for speculators in the oil business, and million dollar deals transpired in the hotel bar, restaurant, and lobby.

She threaded her way through the crowd to the front desk, where she was quickly checked in. She saw a few cowboy hats and Stetsons among the fedoras, but no one was dressed like Will Rogers. Most everyone wore business suits.

A uniformed bellboy led the way to the elevator and showed her to her suite on the third floor. After tipping him and closing the door, she headed to the bathroom to splash cold water on her face and arms.

The charming suite consisted of a sitting room, bedroom, and bath. Sounds of the bustling traffic drifted up through the open window. From this vantage point she could look down Cincinnati and see the layout of the city in neat square blocks. A number of horse-drawn wagons vied for space among the busy motorcar traffic.

A dress didn't seem to be the right choice to barge in on a newsroom full of men, she reasoned as she placed the things from her bags into the bureau drawers. Her knee socks and knickers seemed the better choice. Over her head she pulled on a white middy blouse and tied the navy scarf loosely in the front.

Before leaving the room, she unpacked the Underwood and set it up on the desk in the sitting room, then stepped back to admire the scene. She smiled a little smugly.

Stuffing her keys, a note pad, and pencil into her pocket, she headed out the door. At the last moment, she remembered to retrieve her press card from her purse. She put it in her pocket with the note pad.

The *Tulsa World* offices were a two-block walk down Third Street and then around the corner on Main. She noted a drug store where she could stop on the way back for a cold soda.

Inside the office building, the receptionist on the first floor looked up as Clarette walked in. Clarette handed over her press card, and the girl's eyes grew wider.

"I'm looking for the newsroom," Clarette told her.

"Third floor, ma'am."

Clarette thanked her and hurried toward the elevator.

The busy newsroom on the third floor reminded Clarette of the newsroom at the *New York American,* only on a smaller scale. As she stepped inside the door, she was nearly run over by a tall, broad-shouldered, blond gentleman with the bluest eyes she had ever seen.

"Excuse me, ma'am. I was in a hurry and didn't see you coming in."

"No harm done. I just need a few minutes with one of the reporters, please."

"I'm a reporter. Name's Erik Torsten. What can I do for you?" She noticed his hair was combed back from his face in curly waves. "Not often we have lady visitors up here."

"I'm not actually visiting." She pulled her card out. "I'm on assignment." She sensed the young man stiffening as he took the press card. "I'm from the *New York American* paper, and I'm here to cover the colored uprising."

Suddenly, she knew a wall had gone up between them. The blue eyes burned through her. "Colored uprising?" he said with a snort. "Is that what you Easterners are calling it? What a bunch of bunk." He shoved the card back at her. "I should have known this would happen. But I can't believe they'd send a woman! What's the matter, can't you read the wires we've been sending? We've sent accounts out every day since it happened."

He pointed to the door through which she had just entered. "There are no tidbits for you to pick up around here. So why don't you turn around and go back where you came from?"

# six

Clarette stared at this blue-eyed young Swede as she calculated her next move. He was obviously the same sort as Hank Maxwell, but with a measure more of anger. She'd have to be careful.

"I certainly don't need your help to get a good story," she told him calmly, "but it'd be better for your paper if I had a little cooperation."

He gave a snort. "Sensationalism is all New York is looking for. You come dashing in here and expect in a few short days to understand what's happened here? It's much deeper than that."

Just then, an older man with a beefy face approached them. "Torsten? What's going on over here?"

At his words, Clarette instantly saw some of the air go out of the young man named Torsten. She moved in to take advantage. Extending her card, she turned to the older gentleman and said, "Good morning, sir. I'm from the *New York American*. Sent here on assignment to cover the problems you've had with the colored people."

He took the card and studied her a moment. "Well, well, a woman reporter. What'll they think of next. The times they are a-changing, as they say." He handed back the card and offered a handshake, which she accepted. "Miss Fortier," he said, "I'm Abram Schoggen, editor of this here paper. Welcome to our fine city. I hope your stay here will be a pleasant one. Why don't you come on in my office, and let's talk a spell." He put a hand on her back and ushered her past a row of desks to his office. As he did so, he turned to say, "Torsten, don't you have something you should be doing?"

Clarette heard him answer, "Yes, sir."

Inside the office, the editor motioned her to a chair as he closed the door. From the water cooler in the corner, he filled a paper cup and handed it to her. How did he know she was absolutely parched? Behind him, the wide-open windows looked out on Main Street where not a breath of air was moving. He sat down in a creaky wooden chair on the opposite side of the desk.

"A terrible thing," he said, tugging at his tie. His thick neck seemed to be squeezed into the starched shirt. "Just terrible. Like a nightmare. So many people hurt. Many, many innocent colored people hurt, all because of the ignorance of a few rowdy ones who think they can lick the world. Ones who think that fighting is the only way to make a gain."

Clarette pulled the pad and pencil from her pocket. "What do you mean? What ignorant, rowdy ones? Are you referring to the colored people or the whites?"

"Tulsa is pleased and happy that you big-city reporters are here, and that you care about what happened in our fine city," he said as though he hadn't heard her question. "We'll try to cooperate in any and every way possible."

"Reporters?" She picked up on the plural use of the word.

"You don't think you're the only one, do you?"

She felt horribly naive. Of course she wouldn't be the only one.

"My, my," he said, again shaking his head. "There's a fellow from St. Louis, two from Chicago." He touched one pudgy finger to another as he counted. "Oh yeah, and the one from Cincinnati. But we have nothing to hide. You'll find we're a friendly city. We're glad to help."

The thought of being one in a crowd of many momentarily clouded her thinking, but she struggled to right herself. "I'd like to see some of the back issues of your papers and talk to a few of your staff reporters. . ."

"Oh sure, Miss Fortier. Sure. Anything. We're here to help

you. In fact, you can come here from your hotel tomorrow and we'll just clear a desk for you and give you a little space to work if you'd like. Anything to help. Anything at all."

At one time, Clarette had thought that most all newspaper editors were somewhat alike, but she was wrong. This chief was definitely different.

"Thank you," she said, "but I can work in my hotel room."

"You're staying in the Hotel Tulsa, right? And what do you think of our beautiful hotel, Miss Fortier? Incredible architecture and design. Every bit as good as some of yours in New York, I dare say. Would you agree?"

"The hotel is nice. Very nice." She hadn't come all this way to discuss architecture. "Can you tell me the location of the courthouse and tell me how I can contact the mayor and the police chief?"

Ab slapped his knee and guffawed as though she'd told a good joke. "Now ain't that just something? That's what all them other reporters was asking for. In fact, since all of you are looking for purt' near the same information, we've planned a little get together tonight at the home of Elmore Harland."

"Of the Harland Oil Company?" She felt like biting her tongue as soon as she'd spoken the dumb question. She could hear someone saying: "Oh, Johannes Vanderpool—of the Vanderpool Silks?"

"Harland Oil is only one of a number of oil companies in Tulsa, Miss Fortier. Our Magic City is on its way to becoming the Oil Capital of the world." He paused a moment as though he needed to let this marvelous information sink into her brain. She waited politely.

"I'll call old Elmore and ask him to send a car to the hotel to pick you up. Say seven-thirty?"

Clarette wasn't sure what she was being sucked into, but she felt it would be wise to cooperate, for now anyway. "Seven-thirty is fine, thank you."

He reached for the phone and gave it a couple of clicks. "Operator, give me seven-oh-nine." He looked over at her. "The Harlands are nice people. Just because they have money. . .Oh, hello, Elmore, this is Ab at the *World*. How you doing this morning? Yeah, it is. Mighty hot. And they say no break in sight.

"Say, I have a fine young lady reporter here in my office this morning. She's from the. . ." He paused as he tried to remember. She handed him the card once again. "Oh yeah, I got it right here. *The New York American*." Ab gave her a wink as though they had conspired on the name together. She cringed. What kind of newspaper man was this?

"Her name's Fortier. Miss Clarette Fortier, and she's agreed to come to our little shindig tonight. Could you send a car for her at the hotel at about half past seven? Great. Thanks, Elmore. See you this evening."

He hung up the phone with a kind of finality. "There you go, ma'am. We got you all fixed up." He stood as though everything had been taken care of.

Clarette stood as well. "If you don't mind, I'd like to spend time reading a few files while I'm here. Can you have someone show me around?"

"Well, now that'd be sort of a waste of your time today. No sense in you going over things twice. Why don't you wait until the report is given this evening, and then you'll know what information you still lack. Why, I believe even the mayor is going to be there and give a statement. It'll save you a lot of footwork in this awful heat. What say?"

Somehow, in a vaguely polite way, he was hedging, but she didn't understand why or what to do about it. The man named Erik had vehemently ordered her out, but this editor was politely ordering her out. She wasn't sure which was worse.

"All right, Mr. Schoggen. . ."

"Aw now, we're all home folk around these parts. Just call me Ab. Just plain old Ab." He made his way around the desk and opened the office door. "We'll see you this evening. We'll show you a real Oklahoma welcome." He looked out over the array of desks. "Torsten?"

The blond head looked up from his typewriter. "Sir?"

"See our guest to the elevator, please."

"Yes, sir," he answered as he stood and walk toward them.

Oh great. Just what she needed—a second helping of rancor. Ab pumped her hand one more time, insisting he was so glad she had come. But the tin words were sounding less and less genuine. She let Erik open the door and lead the way down the hall. As they stopped at the elevator, she said, "Mr. Torsten, I understand your dislike at having outsiders converging on your city, but you're a reporter. Wouldn't you do the same thing if you were sent on assignment?"

He shook his head as he gazed up at the elevator dial. He started to speak, then faltered. "I don't know. Maybe." The voice was still icy cold, but the blue eyes had thawed somewhat. Just as she thought he was going to say something, the door clattered open. He shook her hand. "Good day, miss. I hope your stay in Tulsa is a good one." With that he turned on his heel to return to the newsroom.

She was beginning to sense that Erik Torsten was the more genuine of the two. He obviously had deep feelings about the events that had occurred here. But how could she possibly get him to open up to her? Of all the assignments she'd been on, she'd never seen anyone get riled so fast as this tall blond. As she stepped into the hot midday sunshine, she wondered if perhaps she could find Greenwood herself and look over the area alone.

She stopped in at the drug store and climbed on a padded stool at the counter. The soda jerk was a young boy who looked to be in his late teens. After ordering an ice cream soda, she asked him directions to the courthouse and city hall.

"You must be new in town or you'd sure know where the

courthouse is," he said as he set the brimming soda glass in front of her.

"I am new. Just arrived this morning." The sweet ice cream felt nice and cool on her tongue and throat.

From a nearby wire rack, the boy pulled out a city map and unfolded it. "This here's where the courthouse sits, on Fifth Street," he said, pointing to the intersection. "And this here's City Hall at Fourth and Cincinnati. Real easy to find once you know."

The Courthouse was a couple blocks down the street from the *World*, and City Hall was only a block from her hotel. How handy. Nothing like New York City where she walked fifteen or twenty blocks to get where she was going. "Thanks, young man. How much is the map?" She fished in her trouser pocket.

"Nothing at all. The Tulsa Commercial Club wants us to give them out."

"I understand there was a little excitement here a few days ago."

"I guess you mean the riot."

"Were you there? Do you know how it started?"

"There was a whole bunch of people around the courthouse that night. That's why I said if you were from here, you'd know about the courthouse. Some were carrying guns and they were pretty het up about a black boy who had attacked a white girl. The crowd seemed set on getting that boy out of that jail cell. My daddy told me to go on home. Said there was going to be bad trouble."

"I guess your father was right."

"He sure was, ma'am."

Clarette could have asked him what he'd heard from his father about what had happened, but what she didn't need was hearsay from a mere boy. If she needed his information she could always come back. She paid for the soda, thanked him for the map, and returned to the heat of the Tulsa street.

She walked slowly back to Main and then to the courthouse. This, they said, was where the riot had begun. The news clippings she'd read indicated there had been a black man being held in the jail, accused of accosting a white girl. That must have been to whom the soda jerk was referring.

The courthouse was an imposing stone building with triple-arched entrances on two sides and matching arched windows on the second floor. She peered up at the fifth floor where the jail was said to be. Pausing for a moment, she considered going in and asking to talk to the jailer, but she thought better of it. She needed more information first.

Instead, she took Main back to Fourth and turned east to the City Hall where she knew the police department was housed. This would be a better place to begin. Shimmery waves of heat rose up from the sidewalks like mirages in the Sahara. She fanned her face with the folded map as she walked.

Gratefully, she stepped from the heat into the cool interior of city hall. Following the receptionist's instructions, she found the correct door and entered the police headquarters.

A middle-aged man with a droopy black mustache was sitting at the desk. His uniform coat was hanging on a coat rack in the corner. The shirt sleeves of his white shirt were rolled up, and the top button of his shirt was unbuttoned. The brass buttons of his blue vest bulged around his midsection. A whirring wire-faced fan placed on the file cabinet gave little relief from the heat. He looked up as she walked through the door and gave her a smile. "Hello, miss. What can I do for you?"

She brought out her card and let him read it. When he read it, his smile faded. Undaunted, she pressed on. "I'm here on assignment from the *New York American* newspaper. I'd like to ask a few questions about the riot that occurred recently." She'd stopped calling it an "uprising," as it had been first described to her.

"Well now, ma'am, that mess has done been taken care of.

No sense digging around and trying to make trouble."

"I'm not making trouble," she said quickly. "I'm a reporter. I'm looking for facts. Were you on duty that night? Were you at the courthouse?"

"Excuse me just a minute," he said. He rose to his feet, tugging at the necktie. "I'll have to get the chief." He disappeared down the hall, and she could hear voices buzzing. Presently an older man came out. His vest buttons were in a straight row down his middle, and his sleeves were still buttoned at the wrists. He extended his hand. "Miss Fortier? I'm Melvin Dwyer, Chief of Police."

"Pleased to meet you, sir. I'm from the *New York*. . ."

"Yes, I know. From a big city newspaper. I don't know what you folks hope to find here."

"If you have a moment, I'd like to ask you a few questions."

"Sorry, but I don't have a moment. I'm extremely busy just now. There's still a great deal to be done and my force has been working day and night to maintain order after the National Guard troops left town."

"When were the National Guard troops called in and why? Did the governor of the state make that decision?"

He put up his hand. "Please, ma'am. All you folks got all the same questions. Just so you all get the same straight answers we're holding a little get together tonight at. . ."

"I know, I've been told. At the Harland home."

"If you know, then why're you here wasting my valuable time? I'll be there this evening giving all the information you'll need." He turned to go. Over his shoulder, he said. "I'll see you this evening."

So that was that. Back out into the heat. Why, she wondered as she walked back to the hotel, was everyone so elusive? She'd give this thing a chance tonight at the Harland's, then if she wasn't satisfied, she was going to have to take more drastic action.

In her suite, she turned the tub faucets on full blast, ready to cool off in a nice soaking bath. She was startled at the rust-colored water that came out. When the tub was full, there was a layer of dirt on the bottom. *Beautiful town, nice buildings,* she mused as she splashed about in the dirty water, *but still lacking in a number of areas.* She hoped she wouldn't be drinking muddy water. She might have to live on soda pop.

At a quarter past seven, the phone rang. The man at the front desk informed her that her transport had arrived. "I'll be right down," she told him. Probably one of the Harlands' chauffeurs.

"Excuse me, ma'am. He said he'd be right up." And the phone clicked dead. A chauffeur coming up to her room? Now that was strange.

She pulled on her pink cloche which matched her pink chemise and pumps, then grabbed her bag from the desk and moved toward the door just as there was a firm knock.

Opening the door, she was surprised to look into a laughing pair of puppy-brown eyes.

"Hello, Miss Fortier," he said, "welcome to Tulsa. I'm Shelby Harland. But you can call me Shel if you'd like."

## seven

If the son of the oil baron had planned this for a surprise effect, he had succeeded. She was taken off guard, and for a moment was without words. Shelby seemed amused.

"When I learned we had a fine young lady reporter come to town," he said, smiling, "I thought I would come and personally escort you to the goings on at our house. Hope you don't mind."

"No, of course not. I don't mind at all." Frankly, this had been the first truly friendly face she'd seen since arriving. Shelby's smile was open and almost childlike. He was dressed in the loose trousers of an Ivy League man, and his dark jacket, which hung open, complemented his dark hair. After turning the key to lock her door and dropping the key into her bag, she took the arm he offered her as they walked together toward the elevator.

"Ab told Father you were an attractive young lady, but he certainly didn't tell the half," he said, ushering her into the elevator. Strangely, she felt herself blushing—a sensation to which she was unaccustomed. It wasn't his words, which she'd certainly heard before, but it was the air about him. Almost like a child on the verge of a new discovery.

Shelby guided her through the crowded lobby, through the revolving doors, and out into the warm evening. Instead of the staid touring car which she had expected, he opened the door of a silver Kissel speedster. So this was what her father meant when he referred to the "new" oil money out West.

"Do you live right in New York?" he asked after he had helped her in and settled beside her, his shoulder so close to hers she could feel its warmth.

"Brooklyn. Flatbush."

"Ah, but you work in the city. What area?"

"The *American* offices are on Sixth, just south of Broadway."

"I know the area. I love New York."

"Really?" She didn't think many people out West actually liked New York.

He nodded. "My pals from Princeton and I used to spend weekends roaming about the city, going to plays and clubs, and riding on the tops of the buses, just having a good time. I love every inch of New York. It throbs with life."

Clarette had no trouble envisioning Shelby on top a bus. Probably whistling and winking at all the pretty girls. And she agreed with him: New York did throb with life.

She watched the scenery flit by as they drove south out of the city to a residential area. "So you're a Princeton grad?"

"Not yet. I have another year. Dad gave me the choice to either buckle down and study, or drop out until I decide what I want to do."

"And you're busy deciding?"

He turned to her with that mischievous grin. "Yeah. Real busy. Say, I never heard of a woman reporter before. That's quite an achievement, isn't it?"

"I'm not sure if achievement is the right word; I've been kicked around a few times. But I'm making it."

Deftly, he wheeled the Kissel into a driveway. "I'll take you in through the back," he told her. "That's where the crowd's gathering. In the Mendelssohn Room."

"The what?"

"That's what Mother calls it. Rather stuffy, wouldn't you say? Dad calls it the Ridotto Room." He stopped the car in front of a garage that was as spacious as the one on her father's estate, and leaned toward her. "Know what I call it?"

"I've no idea."

He chuckled. "The Jolly Jazz Room."

She laughed with him. "Jazz? You like jazz?"

"Sure."

"And ragtime?"

"Definitely. My pals and I frequented every club in Harlem, ∣stening and learning. It's the only music today."

"Ever been to the Dixie Club?"

"Many times. You?"

"Many times. Small world."

He jumped out to open her door. "Very small."

The Harland house was a three-story red brick colonial which ∣ooked as though there should be sprawling shade trees sur-∣ounding it, as it would have had in New England; however, on ∣his treeless plain, few trees grew at all. From the car, Clarette ∣ould hear the lively music. Shelby took her elbow as they ∣tepped from the drive to the sweeping stone terrace, set about ∣vith hassocks and chaise lounges, and up the steps to the back ∣ntrance.

They passed through an airy screened room that seemed to ∣e an appendage of the terrace, then through a wide arch to the ∣olly Jazz Room, as Shelby called it. Clarette wondered if the ∣ntire town had turned out. Off to the side, a live band was ∣laying pulsating jazz music. Clarette couldn't imagine her par-∣nts having a party with a jazz band playing. But then Ab had ∣alled it a "shindig." Whatever that was.

Shelby dutifully took her around to introduce her to the mayor ∣nd a few city officials. The mayor was a rough-hewn fellow ∣vho appeared to be uncomfortable in a stiff collar and tie. ∣'olice Chief Dwyer was there in full uniform with brass but-∣ons gleaming. Ab Schoggen gave her a nod and a ghost of a ∣mile. Clarette wondered how he could afford such an expen-∣ive tailor-made suit on an editor's salary.

Most of the men were aloof and distant. She wasn't sure if ∣hey resented her being a woman or being a reporter. She then met Mr. and Mrs. Elmore Harland, who seemed quite congenial.

But Shelby didn't tarry long with introductions. He whisked her onto the lighted glass dance floor where she soon realized he loved to dance as much as she. The band was top notch, and they played every song she knew and loved. A number of other young men were in attendance, but she danced only with Shelby. He knew the words to nearly every song and seemed to enjoy singing along as much as he did dancing.

Liquor flowed as though no one had ever heard of Prohibition. Federal agents from New York would have a heyday in this place. By the fourth or fifth dance, and the third cocktail, Clarette nearly forgot what she had come for.

Her watch said after eleven when the mayor made the announcement that all the out-of-town reporters were invited to come down the hall to the Music Room for a briefing.

"Mind if I tag along?" Shelby asked.

"It's your house," she answered, suddenly coming to her senses. She felt almost sheepish as she followed the group, pulling out her note pad and pen as she went. How could she have gotten so caught up with dancing when she should have been finding answers?

Chairs were assembled in neat rows in the Music Room. She pushed through to sit on the front row, anxious to at last get some information on the situation she had come here to find out about. But if she had been disappointed with all the rebuffs she'd received that day, she was even more disappointed in this "briefing."

The mayor and Chief Dwyer addressed the group. In turn, they explained the series of events leading up to the riot. A young bootblack, named Dick Wilson, allegedly tried to accost a white girl in the elevator of a department store, they said. She screamed for help and the boy was arrested. Later that same evening, a group of armed Negroes came to the courthouse to try to get him released.

"I tried to order them to go home," Chief Dwyer explained, "but you know how they get when they're all riled up. Wasn't nothing to do but use force to get them calmed down."

"I heard there was a crowd of whites there as well," one reporter said. "What were they doing there?"

"Just a quiet crowd of spectators and curiosity seekers. That assembly was purely quiet till them colored men, who was armed to the teeth, showed up. Then the scene changed."

A murmur swept through the group. From the back of the room, another question came, "How many people were killed in the ruckus?"

The chief shook his head. "I have no idea. We're still searching through the burned areas for bodies. I suppose maybe thirty or forty people died."

"Thirty or forty blacks or whites?" the same voice asked.

"We're just not sure," the chief answered. "You'll have to give us time."

A man sitting beside Clarette said, "You mentioned burned areas. What was burned and why?"

The mayor again allowed Chief Dwyer to answer. "We were searching for arsenals of weapons. A few places were burned so we could destroy those weapons."

Clarette lifted her hand. "May we tour the area where the riot occurred?"

"Oh no, ma'am. That area is off limits right now. And mighty dangerous over there too, I might add. We believe a few hold-out snipers are still in hiding. There are still field orders that no whites go into the area until we're certain all the rioters have been stilled."

The man beside her, whom she later learned was from the *Cincinnati Enquirer*, said, "I understand you still have the Negro men interned at various points in the city. Where are these internment centers?"

"Again, gentlemen," he said, "and lady," he added nodding to Clarette, "you must understand this is has been like a war. We don't know yet who the rabble rousers are in the group. That's why we were forced to round up many in order to find the few. We'd ask that you stay back out of the way and let our police and other officials complete the work that needs to be done at this time."

"If you're interested," the mayor put in, mopping his brow as he spoke, "tomorrow we'll take you to a number of the aid sites where relief supplies are being distributed. It's our aim to protect, and alleviate the suffering of, all the innocents from the Greenwood area as soon as possible."

The mayor's raspy voice softened as he added, "We are intensely humiliated by this terrible tragedy and we pledge every effort to wiping out the stain of it at the earliest possible moment. We're doing everything possible to bring the guilty parties to justice. We ask that you be understanding of us as we go about our work."

With that little speech, the group was dismissed, but they were reminded there was still plenty of good food, good liquor, and good music for the remainder of the evening. Clarette turned to the man from the *Enquirer*. "Are you going on that tour tomorrow?"

He folded his notebook and stuck it in his coat pocket. "Naw. It's pretty clear to me they aren't giving out any more info than absolutely necessary. They're covering up mountains, and everyone here knows it. I'm phoning these notes in tonight, and clearing out of here tomorrow. It may be hot in Cincinnati, but not this hot." He stood to his feet and looked around the room with eyes of total boredom. "If you're smart, lady, you'll do the same."

"What do you think they're covering up?"

He looked at her with an empty stare. "Have you ever seen an out-of-control mob?"

She shook her head.

"I didn't think so. Who sent you on this job, anyway? For your future reference, a mob sorta goes crazy. Then later everyone's real sorry and real embarrassed. Especially if there's a bunch of respectable folk involved. But they'll keep saying they didn't do anything wrong. If they say it long enough, pretty soon the whole town will believe it."

"So why doesn't someone just find out the truth?"

He shook his head as his eyes rolled heavenward. "Lady," he said, jabbing a finger at her, "listen good. People who are hiding something get very touchy when someone comes along and tries to uncover it. Frankly, I care more about my life than that. I got a wife and a couple kids." He slapped a hat on his head and touched the brim. "See you around—reporter." He gave a silly laugh.

*Let him laugh*, she thought as she watched him stride out of the room. She hadn't come all this way to give up so easily.

Shel came up beside her. "Most of these guys are leaving town tomorrow. Will you be leaving, too?"

"I'm not sure."

He took her arm as they followed the group back to the Jazz Room where the music had again started up a lively two-step beat. "Another dance?" He waved to the dance floor where pink, yellow, and blue lights blinked on and off in soft waves beneath the thick-paned glass floor.

"Thanks, but I think I'm ready to return to the hotel if you don't mind." Clarette's desire to dance had waned. She wanted a good night's sleep so she'd be fresh the next morning. She still had work to do here. Others might be satisfied with this thin amount of information, but she was not.

"I'll tell Dad we're leaving," Shelby told her. She waited by the door until he was again by her side to escort her to the car. As they drove back down Main Street, Shel was humming one of the dance melodies. He looked over at her. "I get the feeling you weren't satisfied with the briefing tonight."

"It didn't amount to much." She didn't want to say what she was really thinking. "By the way, Shel, where were you the night of the riot? Did you see anything?"

"Not me. I was safe at home. Guns scare me. In fact, Mom and I hid our nigras and a few of their friends and families in our basement. But for heaven's sake, don't tell Chief Dwyer."

"No, of course I won't." Suddenly Shel seemed a bit more interesting. "How long did you hide them?"

"Just a day or so. We didn't want to break the law, we only wanted to keep them from harm. Colored people need to be taken care of, you know. Sort of like little children. Sometimes they need to be saved from themselves." He pulled up in front of the hotel and stopped the car. "When the order came prohibiting the use of servants' quarters for any other nigras than those employed, we turned the others over to the authorities. But our own servants were safe, thank goodness."

"What happened to those you turned out?"

He shrugged. "Interned with the others, I suppose. I certainly didn't follow along to see." He studied her face and smiled. "Look, you're probably not interested in visiting the aid stations tomorrow. Am I right?"

"I don't think I'll learn anything of value there. I could go there later. I want to see the riot area."

"That's what I figured. As the chief said, it's strictly off limits, but I could give you a looksee from a distance. You won't even have to get your pretty self dirty."

"Would you do that?"

"For such a great dancer as you? I sure would."

"You're not such a bad dancer yourself," she told him. It had been a gay evening, even though she hadn't learned much. She rather liked going to a shindig.

As he walked her to the lobby, she said, "Don't bother seeing me to my room. What time shall I expect you tomorrow?"

"How about ten? Then we can come back here and have lunch. You'll love the food in this restaurant. It's the greatest."

"Fine. See you then."

*Finally*, she thought as she stepped into the elevator. Now maybe she could learn what had really happened here.

# eight

Even though she knew Sid was probably still at the news office into the wee hours, she opted to wait till morning to call him. She didn't trust the effects of the cocktails. When she did put through the long distance call the next morning at about eight, she found him anxious to hear from her.

"Where you been, kid? I thought you'd call in right away. Whatcha got?"

"Not much so far, Chief." She spread her notes out on the desk in front of her. "The locals here are pretty closed-mouthed."

"I don't doubt it. Sounds like it was an ugly mess. Lot of vigilante activity in the area, from what I understand. Those kind usually try to cover their tracks. They still playing wild West cowboys out there?"

"Looks that way."

"Have you heard about a lynching that took place only a few days prior to the riot?"

She pulled her note pad close and poised her pencil. "Not a word. Tell me more."

"Just got the info late last night from a reliable source. Some black kid by the name of Jasper Franklin. See if you can find out more about him. Maybe that's why the blacks were up in arms."

"Jasper Franklin. Got it." She wrote quickly as he spoke. "I'll look into it. The city officials held a briefing for reporters last evening and I was there, but the information they gave consisted mostly of what we already know." She read him most of her notes, which were quite brief.

"What about the *World* office?"

"I was politely ushered out, but I'm going back over there later this afternoon."

"I'll probably rue the day I sent a dame on this assignment," he muttered. "Well, if you can't get any cooperation with the *World*, go ahead and visit the *Tribune's* office as well. Maybe they'll be more congenial."

"Will do. I'm being driven to where I can see the destruction this morning. The area is policed and is off limits, but this fellow says he can take me to where I can see it. He's coming to pick me up shortly."

"A fellow? Now listen, Fortier, don't be getting any romantic notions while you're out there. Keep your mind on your business."

Clarette felt like a kid caught with her hand in the cookie jar. She did think that Shel was a nice guy. Fun, polite, accommodating, accomplished dancer, nice singing voice, and such a great smile. "Don't worry," she assured him. "My mind is on business."

"Remember, we ain't made out of money. Hurry and get this thing sewed up."

"Right, Chief. I'll do my best."

Clarette would have liked to have worn a dress that morning, but she let wisdom win out and wore her trousers. But even dressed in the tweed trousers, middy, and loafers, she received a look of approval from Shel when he appeared at her door.

"That's a nifty outfit," he told her, giving her his wide smile. "You all ready?"

"Just let me grab the camera and film bag," she told him.

He stepped inside as she went to the bedroom to retrieve the bag and camera. When she came back out to the sitting room, he was admiring the Underwood. "I thought about getting one of these if I go back to school next fall. How do you like it?"

"Love it." She showed him how the lid fit on to make the handy carrying case. "I've turned out reams of copy on this little jewel. By the way, I need a package of typing paper. I left in such a hurry, I had no time to purchase any. Is there a stationer's store in the area?"

"Right down the street. I'll show you after lunch."

"Thanks. You're a great help."

"Anything at all," he said as he ushered her down the hall-way. "Anything at all."

Mounds of puffy white clouds hung in the blue sky. Clarette studied them as they drove along a dusty road north of the city. The wide open spaces were a source of fascination to her. Even in rural New Jersey the horizon was filled up with tree-covered hills. She was totally unaccustomed to seeing this much sky at one time. Shadows raced across the road in front of them as the sun dipped in and out behind the puffs of clouds.

When reading history books about the westward migration of pioneers across this great land, she used to wonder what pulled them. The newness and freshness of this place was beginning to give her a glimpse of why. She sensed the thrill of discovery, the thrill of being the first person in a place. Putting down roots and building a new town on a naked prairie. How exciting that must have been. And now the discovery of rich oil pumping out of the earth. What a fertile land this was.

As the purring Kissel made its way up a hill, she could see even further out across the prairie. Something about the wind blowing through the tall grass made her pulse race. She couldn't quite grasp what it was that excited her so.

"You ever been in Tulsa before?" Shelby asked, breaking the comfortable silence.

"Never. I've never even been this side of the Mississippi." She started to name a few of the places where she'd visited, but suddenly remembered her masquerade as a working girl.

"Big difference from back East, would you say?"

"I would indeed."

"My dad says people usually either hate this place or love it.

No middle ground. Where will you fit?"

"The latter, I think."

He grinned at her. "Honest? I never would have thought it." He paused. "On second thought, any gal with grit enough to make it as a reporter probably would take to this rough and tumble place." He steered the car around a tight curve as they came up the side of a hill. "If you'd lived about fifty years ago, you might have been like Calamity Jane, toting a six-shooter and riding a wild pony."

She laughed at the thought. Maybe she would have. In fact, it sounded rather tempting. As they crested the top of the hill, Shelby pulled off the road and parked. The city lay spread out before them. "This is called Standpipe Hill. You wanted to see, and this seemed to be the best place to give you a look." He pointed off to their left. "There it is. There's where the riot took place."

As she turned to look that direction, she gave an involuntary gasp at the sight. There were blocks and blocks of nothing but smoldering ruins. How could this be? Without waiting for Shelby, she got out and walked to the brink of the hill for a better look. "I can't believe this. I thought there was just a small area burned. This is unbelievable. What happened? How could there have been this much destruction?"

Suddenly he was beside her. He touched her arm. "Now, Clarette, don't get upset. You heard what the Chief Dwyer said last evening. There wasn't anything else they could do. They did what they had to do to bring peace and order to the area."

She shivered in the hot sunshine. "But this. . .people's houses. Homes. Where are the people now? They have no homes."

"Well now, that's what the relief aid stations are for. That's where they're giving out needed food and supplies."

She turned to look at him to be sure he was serious. "Food and supplies? That's like putting an umbrella up in a wind gale. Just from this one observation I can see more is needed than food and supplies."

Suddenly remembering, she ran back to the car to get the camera and opened the bellows. "Help me with the drape, will you, Shel?" she asked. "I'll need to block out this bright sunlight."

How she wished she had a moving picture camera. Carefully, she pressed the camera to her midsection, and focused the scene before her through the ground-glass window. As Shel assisted her with the black drape, she was able to get several shots. At this distance the details wouldn't be very clear, but this was the best she could do for now. Now, more than ever, she wanted to get into that area.

"What about the Negroes who work at your place, Shel?"

"What about them? I told you we hid them that night. They know little or nothing about what happened."

"But surely they have friends and family. May I interview your Negro workers?"

Shelby took off his hat and wiped his brow with the back of his hand. "First of all, I don't think Dad would like that. But secondly, they have quarters at our home. They may have friends in Greenwood, but they don't live in Greenwood. It would just be a waste of your time."

His logic made sense. Still there had to be a way to learn more. "I'm going to the police station to try to get a permit to go into the area," she told him as they returned to the car.

"As I understand it, Chief Dwyer has deputized about a hundred members of the American Legion. Those men are armed and stationed all around the area. Not only that, the National Guard are still on standby. Now with all that artillery, it's certainly no place for a lady to be."

"But you're talking to Calamity Jane. Remember?"

As they drove back into the city, she realized she needed to be alone to get the things done that needed to be done. As much as she enjoyed being with Shel, having lunch with him was out of the question.

"Now I am disappointed," he confessed. "I was looking forward to spending the time with you. I'm enjoying getting to know you."

"I appreciate all your kindness, but I must keep my mind on business. I'd better spend this afternoon writing up as much copy as I can."

"I understand. What about dinner this evening? I could come to the hotel."

She shook her head. "No thanks. If you remember, I was up quite late last evening. I need my rest."

"Okay then, I'll try for tomorrow night. After you're rested. What do you say?"

"Give me a call tomorrow and I'll let you know."

"It's a deal."

He found a parking place near the hotel and jumped out to open her door. Helping her out, he said, "Say, don't forget you need typing paper. There's a stationer's shop down the street about a block. I'll walk you there."

Clarette repressed a sigh of frustration. He was right, she did need the paper, but she was anxious to get over to the police department. She thanked him and fell into step beside him. He was humming a lilting melody as they walked along.

She couldn't remember ever meeting a nicer man than Shelby. Had circumstances been different, she would have liked to have spent more time with him. Perhaps he'd return to Princeton and next winter she could meet him in New York and they'd have a gay time dancing away the hours in the best clubs.

She purchased new ink nibs and pencils, as well as the paper, and Shelby carried the package for her back to the hotel. On the way, he tried his best to talk her into at least having a cold ice cream soda with him, but she remained adamant.

At last, she was in her room, and Shelby had departed. She let a few minutes lapse by splashing her face and arms with

cool water and running a brush through her short dark curls.
Firming the broad-brimmed hat back on her head, she was back
on the street—looking first to make sure his car was gone. Confident he was nowhere in sight, she hurried off in the direction
of city hall.

When she found herself standing in the same office that she'd
stood in the day before, she wondered why she'd been so confident. The same sergeant gave her the same blank look and called
once again for Chief Dwyer to come and talk to her.

He reiterated what Shelby had said. "I have armed men posted
throughout the area," he said, "and they're skittish as a new colt
at daybreak. Absolutely no way am I gonna be responsible for
some daft female who gets into the wrong place at the wrong
time and gets herself hurt."

"But I'll take full responsibility. I'll even sign a paper stating
that I'm doing so."

"Look, ma'am, I took time last evening to address all the
reporters so all of you would have the same information. I didn't
have to do that. I'm a busy man. I've had precious few hours of
sleep since this thing hit last week. I'm mighty short on patience and if you continue to rile me, I'm likely to kick you out
just like I would if you were a man."

If he was bluffing, it was a good bluff. She didn't think it
would pay to press the matter further. Back on the hot street,
she once again considered walking to Greenwood. But then what
would she do when she got there? Who could she talk to? And
where would she find anyone in all that devastation?

It seemed hopeless. She might just as well pack and go home.
But instead of heading back to the hotel, she turned toward Main.
She'd try the *World* once more. At least they understood her
need for the full story.

As she stepped into the lobby, she breathed in the good smells
from the coffee shop. She pulled off her hat and fanned her face
with it. She couldn't remember ever being this hot. A glass of

lemonade would certainly taste good. She'd only stop for a minute. As she pulled open the door to the coffee shop, she felt a bit of resistance. She gave a sharp tug and heard a grunt from the other side. There stood the big Swede with a paper cup of dripping sloshed coffee in his hand.

"Quite a grip you have there, Miss Fortier."

"Excuse me." He must have grabbed the door at the same moment she had been tugging it open. She stepped to a nearby table to fetch a paper napkin to hand to him.

"Thank you." He mopped coffee off his hand.

"Did you burn yourself?"

He shook his head. "I don't know why I keep drinking this hot stuff, anyway."

"All reporters are addicted to coffee," she quipped.

"Speaking of all reporters, I thought you'd be gone by now, along with everyone else. Didn't you sit in on that neat little briefing last night and get your canned story?"

She caught the cynicism in his voice. "I not only got the canned story, but I also saw the burned-out area of Greenwood from Standpipe Hill."

"Don't tell me. Let me guess. You were taken on that grand tour of the hilltop view by someone by the name of Harland."

She was startled. "How did you know that?"

He gave a dry laugh. "Old Shelby Harland is ready and willing to help any damsel in distress. In fact, sometimes they don't even have to be in distress."

This blond giant was about to get on her nerves. "Look, I don't care what you think about this guy. At least he's been civil, which is more than I can say for you. Excuse me please while I rest my burning feet and order a lemonade. Can I buy you one?" She walked to a booth, hoping against hope that he would follow. He did.

# nine

After he was seated across from her, and the tall glass of iced lemonade was nursing her burning throat, she said, "There's more here, isn't there? You hinted at it yesterday when I first came in the door."

"What do you care? Your chief wants to hear what he wants to hear and you've got a job to do. Why don't you just do it and get on back to the big city?"

"I want to know what really happened."

"You wouldn't have the courage to write it if you learned it."

"Why do you say that? Because you don't?" As soon as she'd said it, she knew it was a knockout blow. It gave her no pleasure, though. The stricken look that crossed his face stunned her.

He was quiet for a moment. The clear blue eyes were looking past her, not only in space but possibly in time as well. "Do you really want into Greenwood?" he asked.

"Can you get me there?"

"You answer me first."

"Yes, I do."

"Then yes—I can." He finished the last of his lemonade. "I hope you're ready for this." He walked with her out into the lobby. "Where're you staying?"

"At the Hotel Tulsa."

"I'll be by to pick you up in the morning at seven-thirty."

"Why so early?"

He gave her an intense look. "Because it's before Shelby Harland gets out of bed."

Some problem was obviously between these two, but it didn't

76

concern her. "I'll be ready."

"And please—don't tell anyone what you're doing."

"I won't. I promise. And thanks."

"You may not be thanking me before this is all over."

Afraid to ask what he meant, she hurriedly left and returned to her room.

She ate a light supper in the hotel restaurant and then called Sid.

"So when are you leaving to come back?" was his first question.

"Can you give me more time, Sid? I'm on to something."

"On to something. Now what's that supposed to mean? Sounds like a dime novel."

"Tomorrow morning I'm going into the Negro area called Greenwood."

"You said the area was under guard. Off limits."

"It is. I've met a reporter from the *World* who's agreed to take me in."

"And how does he get in?"

"I don't know for sure. I'll find out tomorrow. Sid, I saw the area from a nearby hilltop today and it's a bigger area than you could imagine. Bigger than any of the reports have indicated—and it's lying in rubble. It's unbelievable."

"Yeah? So? What happens when you get in?" His tone was getting more exasperated.

"First of all, I'll get close-up photos. But better than photos, I'll be able to talk to the ones who went through the riot."

"Melodramatic dames," she heard him mutter.

"Sid, can you give me another week here?"

"A week?" The words exploded through the phone. She held the receiver away from her ear. "What are you, crazy? You think this newspaper is made of money?"

"I think I can get you some exclusives, but I'll need more time. How about it, Sid?"

"Four more days. That's all. Four days."

"Four days. You got it, Chief. Thanks."

"And you better be sending info to me each day."

"I'll do it. Thanks, Chief. You'll not regret it."

"Kid, I'm already regretting it."

That night Clarette heard the gentle patter of rain through her open hotel window. The pleasant sound made her thankful. Possibly it would settle the dust and bring down the temperature. But then she thought of all the people in Greenwood and all the burned homes. She lay awake staring at the ceiling, wondering if they had shelters over their heads against the rain.

She was up early the next morning to make sure she had full boxes of film for the camera, extra pencils, and paper. At seven-thirty on the nose, Erik called her from the downstairs hotel phone to let her know he had arrived—unlike Shelby who came right on up to her room.

When the elevator door opened, he was standing waiting for her, looking much different than her original impression of him. He was more relaxed and a hint of a smile played on his lips.

"I would have laid a bet that you wouldn't be ready," he said.

"I get up much earlier than this to catch the subway in Brooklyn to get to work in New York," she told him, slinging the strap of her film bag over her shoulder. He reached out to take the camera from her.

"Have you had breakfast?" He nodded toward the restaurant.

"No, but I don't need anything. Let's get going."

"I was in New York once," he said as he led her out to the street.

"Oh yeah? When?" At the curb was a Model T. She should have guessed Erik would have a Model T. It was a nice one, but a Model T nonetheless.

He opened her door. She stepped on the running board and got in. "We shipped out from New York, and then docked there on our way back from France during the war," he said as he seated his large frame behind the wheel. He seemed to fill the entire car. "I didn't get to see much on the way out, but coming back, my buddies and I took time to see the sights before we left."

"Did you like it?"

"New York? It was all right. Sure is big and crowded. I felt sorta boxed in."

"After being used to the wide open prairie, I can see why." She studied his broad hands on the steering wheel. "Where were you during the war?"

"France. Champagne. I was with the Tulsa Ambulance Company."

"And you saw a lot of fighting?"

"I saw a lot of dead and wounded," he commented flatly.

He steered the chugging car east on Third for a ways before turning north on Elgin. The city was quiet this early in the morning. The coolness she'd hoped for from the rain had not materialized. Instead, the air had been transformed into a steam bath. The air was now hot and damp, rather than just hot. At intervals, she saw the deputized men standing guard. The sight of them gave her an odd sensation. She wondered if they had been part of the riot.

"I thought I'd seen all the war I was ever going to see," he said, his voice quiet and thoughtful. "Until this."

"Where were you the night it all happened?" she asked him.

He looked over at her. How she wished she could read into his clear blue eyes. "I was gone. Out of town. On business, I guess you could say."

"Fortunate for you."

"Yeah. Fortunate."

The Model T's motor slowed as they approached a guard standing in the middle of the street. He had no uniform, was dressed like a ordinary citizen, but a shiny badge was fastened to the lapel of his jacket.

"Hey there, Torsten."

"Morning, Jack. I'm taking a few things to Tessa." He fished in his pocket, pulled out a green card, and waved it. The words "Police Protection" were printed in black letters on the card.

The man named Jack was cradling a shotgun. Clarette assumed he knew how to use it. The guard nodded at the card, then peered across Erik to where she was sitting. "Who you got there?"

"This is a friend of mine," Erik said, jerking his thumb at her.

Jack grinned. "Aw, you young pups are all alike. New girl every week." He stepped back to let the Model T chug on down the street.

The acrid stench of charred burning hung like a pall in the moist air. Even after a week, the smell was almost overpowering. Clarette saw, but her mind could not comprehend what she was seeing. It was too terrible to fathom. The sidewalks were there. Driveways were there. But house after house was burned to the ground. Here and there, bits of charred building frame leaned precariously, ready to fall at the slightest wind. An iron bedstead was a ghostly reminder that a person had lived there just a few short days earlier. A few canvas tents had been erected as makeshift shelters.

From the few houses that had been spared, or partially spared, Clarette could see they were modest frame homes, similar to the ones in the neighborhood where she lived in Brooklyn. What had she thought? That they were a few little shanties on the outskirts of a town? She wasn't sure now what she'd thought, but nothing like this.

Erik pulled the car to a stop. His voice startled her. "You gonna take pictures?"

"Yes. Yes, I am." Wouldn't this show Sid a thing or two? She stood beside the car, loaded the Graflex, and began aiming and shooting. "Where are we going?" she asked as she climbed back in.

"I don't want to drive around too much just now. No sense in drawing attention to you. Everyone's still jittery. We'll go see my cousin first, then I'll show you what's left of the business district."

"There's a business district?"

"There *was* a business district."

She let that comment soak in a minute. "When you told the guard that you were coming in to see someone, you really meant it?"

Turning the Model T down another street, he nodded. "I meant it."

"What's your cousin doing here?"

"I'll let her tell you that."

At the end of the street they were on sat a house that was partially burned on the front, but with the rear still intact. Erik parked out front. "She'll probably be in here, since it's still early."

Suddenly, in a momentary panic, Clarette didn't know if she could go through with this. In spite of her brassy exterior, she felt like scooting over to the driver's seat and speeding out of there as fast as the Model T would take her. Herta was right that her life had been protected and sheltered. But it was too late. She'd come this far.

Erik helped her out, then retrieved a bag from behind the seat. He led her across blackened grass around to the back yard. There stood a black woman standing over a cooking fire. She was stirring something in a cast iron kettle. It smelled rather good.

"Hey, Chloe. How's it going?"

The black woman looked up from her cooking and gave a bright smile. "How-do, Mister Erik. Lordy, what you doing bringing more fixin's in that bag?"

"I figured you could use more. Did the Pattons let you have a day off work?"

"Shows how much you know, Mister Erik. This here's my

regular day off."

Erik grinned and it was the first time Clarette had seen a full smile on his face. It was an arresting smile that spread across the fair cheeks and lit up the soft blue of his eyes. "You're right, Chloe, I don't know much. Is Tessa up?"

"She is. That gal ain't hardly slept a wink since the big ruckus. She be right there in the kitchen. Ain't you gonna mind your manners now and introduce me to your lady friend here?"

Erik turned to Clarette as though he'd forgotten he'd brought her along. He gave a soft flustered laugh. "Sorry. Chloe, this is Clarette Fortier. She's a reporter from New York City."

"My, my. That's a mighty fer piece to be comin' from. New York City." She said the words over as though she were tasting the sound of them.

Clarette stepped over to the woman and extended her hand. "Pleased to meet you, Chloe." The black woman wiped her hand on her apron and returned the handshake.

"Wish I could offer you better hospitality, but we're in a bit of a fix just now, as you can see."

*A bit of a fix?* That was an interesting way to describe it. "Don't worry about that," Clarette assured her. "I just want to ask you a few questions."

"What's all the talking out here?" came a voice from the screened-in porch. Clarette watched as a miniature female replica of Erik walked out the door and down the steps. She had the same clear blue eyes and cornsilk-color hair. Only this tiny girl, who stood barely five feet tall, had her hair in braids which were wound around the top of her head. Almost like a golden halo. She wore a simple cotton dress that appeared to be home-made. Her arm bore a pure white bandage and hung in a sling.

Erik quickly introduced her as his cousin, Tessa Jurgen. "Tessa was right here during the worst of the riot," Erik explained.

"Well, not here exactly," Tessa said. "Actually I was down there." Clarette looked as she pointed to a house down the street that was standing intact. "My fiancé and I hid in the basement." There was a hint of a Swedish lilt to her speech. "Chloe said she felt it wouldn't be torched since it belonged to a white man, and she was right."

Clarette had fished her pad and pencil from her pocket. "What happened to your arm, Miss Jurgen?"

"Sniper bullet done got her." Chloe offered the answer. "When we was getting her and her beau snuck down into that cellar, she got shot."

Clarette felt a shudder go through her. *Being shot at. That was pretty heady stuff. Stuff that happened to soldiers and gangsters, not pretty little girls.* "What were you doing here, Miss Jurgen? In the colored section of town?"

"It's sort of a long story." Tessa rubbed her wounded arm with her hand. "If you don't mind me asking, why do you want to know?"

"Clarette wants to hear the side of the story that's not been told yet," Erik explained.

Tessa glanced over at Chloe and then shook her head. "I'm not sure it'll do any good."

"Why? What do you mean?" Clarette asked.

"People hear what they want to hear and believe what they want to believe. You can't change that."

"Maybe not, but I also can't change the fact that I'm compelled to uncover the truth. Miss Jurgen. . ."

"Please. My students call me that. Just call me Tessa."

*Students? This little thing has students?* "Tessa then. My boss in New York is screaming at me to get out of here and get back home. My expense money is almost gone. But I wasn't satisfied with what I've learned from the police, the mayor. . ." She shot a withering look at Erik. "Or the city newspapers."

Tessa nodded as though she understood. "Come on in and sit down."

"Not long," Erik said. "I need to get her out of here before we arouse the suspicion of those crazy guards."

"Have Mama Sue fetch them bowls," Chloe said to Tessa as the girl turned to go inside. "This here oatmeal's nigh on to being fit to eat."

Inside the roomy kitchen a number of black women were milling about. Past the kitchen Clarette could see where large colorful quilts had been strung up to hide the burned areas and to afford privacy. At the kitchen table sat a young girl who was nursing a tiny baby, who, Clarette learned, had come into the world the night of the riot.

A rotund lady named Mama Sue flashed a wide, bright smile when she was introduced. "Hey there, sugar. Now you just come on in here and make yourself at home. Don't mind we got a little mess around here." She patted the blue bandanna which was wrapped turban-like around her head. "We wasn't exactly 'specting no company. You need to talk to Miss Tessa—we let you two come on in here." She led the way to the front room where the quilts hung. Against one wall, still intact, was an old upright piano and a matching claw-leg stool.

"If you don't mind," Clarette said, seating herself on the couch, "I'd like to talk to you women as well."

Mama Sue gave a hearty laugh. "Ain't no problem there, sugar. We be talking all the time."

Clarette was given a bowl of oatmeal and a spoon. Even though she felt as steamy hot as the cereal, she remembered she'd skipped breakfast. Mama Sue brought her own bowl and sat down on the couch beside Clarette. Three of the other women dragged in kitchen chairs and set them about the room. Tessa sat on the floor with her legs tucked under her, looking like a child.

Clarette managed to eat and take notes in intervals as the women told of that night of terror, explaining how they'd tried to hide from the gunfire and later on how the rioters had begun setting fire to the houses and massively looting.

"We run to our big new church," Mama Sue said. "My husband, Preacher Sam, he be the pastor there. But they done burn us out there too. Wasn't nothing we could do then."

"But what set it off? I understand there were Negro men who were downtown with guns."

"Shouldn't have been no guns," Mama Sue said, suddenly serious. "Me and Preacher Sam told 'em and told 'em—no guns. You only get hurt bad, Preacher told 'em. But they wouldn't listen. They was fighting mad."

"Over what? I've been told there was a lynching before this incident with the bootblack boy ever happened. Is that true?"

Mama Sue nodded. "That's the truth, sugar. Uh-huh. That's what happen all right. That's why our men were all up in arms. They set it in their minds that it ain't never gonna happen again."

"Tell me about the lynching," Clarette said. "What happened?"

"Chloe," Tessa called to the woman who was still out in the kitchen. "Can you come in here?"

"I's coming, child." Chloe stuck her head around the door frame. "What y'all want?"

"You can ask her," Tessa waved toward Chloe.

"Ask Chloe about the lynching? Was she there?" Clarette asked.

"She wasn't there," Tessa said. "It was her son who was hanged."

# ten

Suddenly the heat in the room became stifling. Clarette wondered if her oatmeal was going to stay down. From the lamp table beside her, she picked up a cardboard fan with a wooden handle. On one side was a picture of Jesus holding a soft, wooly lamb in His arms. On the other side was an advertisement for a local funeral home. She fanned her face and tried to catch her breath.

Chloe came and sat on the piano stool, tears forming in her dark eyes at the mention of her son.

"Why?" Clarette asked. "Why would they. . ."

From the doorway, Erik spoke. "We better go now. We've stayed as long as we can."

"Just another minute, please," she told him.

"They had no call to hang my boy," Chloe was saying. "No call. They say he touched a white girl. But my Jasper wouldn't. He wouldn't." Her hands were folded in the lap of her dress and she rocked back and forth as she spoke. "He was just ready to graduate from high school."

"What white girl? Where?" Clarette was writing furiously.

Tessa answered for her since Chloe was unable to continue. "The girl's name is Sadella Patton."

"Any relation to the Patton Oil Company family?"

"Their daughter," Tessa told her. "I worked for the family, tutoring the younger children."

"You know them personally? Can you get me an interview?"

Tessa shook her head. "They've washed their hands of me. Besides, they're away on summer holiday."

"Clarette," Erik said again with a warning sound to his voice.

She stood to her feet. "All right. All right." She looked around at the circle of serene faces. In the light of all that had happened, how could they be this calm? "Thank you all so much." She went to Chloe and touched her shoulder. "I'm very sorry about your son." Chloe responded with a nod.

Clarette then turned to Mama Sue and reached out for her hand. "Thanks for the breakfast."

"Shucks, sugar. Weren't nothing. If you'd a been here afore all this mindless ruckus, I'd a fixed you a big old scrumptious mess of hotcakes, grits, and the works."

"I'm sure you would have."

"Mind you, sugar," the hefty lady said as she pushed against the couch to stand up. "The Klan ain't gonna take kindly to y'all talking to us here. You know that, don't you?"

"The Ku Klux Klan?" Clarette had heard of the Klan, but she hadn't really thought of them being mixed up in all this.

"They think they's pretty big stuff around these here parts. Course they ain't nothing next to the power of Almighty God. But still, you gotta watch out and step careful."

"I will, Mama Sue. Thanks again."

Quietly she followed Erik out to the car. Neither of them spoke as he drove the Model T around a different way to show her the ruins of the business district. It was as disheartening to see as the residential area. The entire space of several blocks was burned out. Dozens of once-thriving businesses were leveled. Brick shells testified that these had been solid, well-built stores, shops, and offices.

"I never imagined the business district would be so. . .so large."

Erik nodded. "It's known around the country as 'Black Wall Street.' Many of the blacks here are quite prosperous. I should say, they were." He stopped at intervals so she could step out and take photos of the area.

Clarette was more than ready to return to her Underwood and get to work. "Do you go over there every day?" she asked him as he parked the Model T in front of the hotel.

He was quiet for a time. "You want to go back?"

"I need to know more about what happened at the courthouse. How can I talk to a few of the men?"

Erik hooked his wrist over the steering wheel as he turned to look at her. His sandy brows came together in a scowl. "The menfolk are either dead, injured, or interned. Not many are available."

"She mentioned Preacher Sam."

"I think they've allowed him to come and go some. Maybe he has to report back to the internment center at night, I don't know for sure."

"May I go to one of the centers? Where are they?"

"They've moved them a couple of times. Most are at the fairgrounds as far as I know. But you won't be able to get in there. It's sewed up tight."

"How about the hospital?"

"Miss Fortier. . ."

"Clarette."

Erik cleared his throat softly. "Clarette. I appreciate what you're trying to do. In fact, I see now that you do care about what's going on here, and I apologize for my outburst the other day when you first arrived."

"Oh, that's all right. I. . ."

He lifted his hand. "Let me finish. Please understand you've come into a sticky situation here."

"That's an understatement."

"The men who have a vigilante mindset think they're above the law. They firmly believe what they're doing is right. The Bible calls it 'deception.' They've deceived themselves. Because they're deceived—because they're convinced they're right—they have no conscience."

Clarette couldn't see what this had to do with her. "Would you mind telling me what you're getting at?"

"Just this. If you write a few humdinger stories for your New York paper, and the hate-filled individuals find out who talked to you, they could be targeted for retaliation."

"They could get hurt?" She thought of Mama Sue and those women who'd gathered in her house.

He nodded. "But that's not all. If they don't like what you're doing, they'll try to stop you as well."

"They're that powerful?"

"You cannot even imagine how powerful."

"But someone's got to stop them."

A slight smile played on his lips. "Be hanged if you don't sound like Tessa."

Clarette doubted she had much in common with the pretty blond girl in the homemade dress. "In what way?"

"The day before Jasper Franklin was hanged, that little half pint walked right through the crowd at the courthouse and visited the boys in the jail. That's how she lost her job with the Pattons. They warned her to stay away from the colored folks, but Tessa wouldn't listen." Admiration sounded in his voice.

"What a spitfire."

"It's her faith in God that makes her that way."

Now Clarette was sure they had nothing in common. Time to change the subject. "You said 'boys.' I thought only one was lynched."

Erik's expression clouded; a muscle twitched in his square jaw. "Only one was lynched," he said quietly.

"How many were arrested?"

"Two that day."

"What happened to the other one?"

He hesitated. "They. . .I heard he escaped somehow."

"Escaped a mob?"

"He was a big fellow. Just a boy, but big. They call him Strapper."

"Where would he have gone?"

Erik shrugged his wide shoulders. "Across the border into Arkansas most likely." He obviously knew more about this deal than he was telling, and she wanted to know what it was. But he evaded her by saying, "You'll have to excuse me if I don't walk you inside, but I need to get over to the office before Ab has my hide."

"I'm sorry. I almost forgot." She grabbed her camera and bag. "One more thing. Do you know where I can get my photos developed?"

"I could do it."

"You?"

"My buddy Gaven MacIntyre—Tessa's fiancé—he and I have been messing around with a darkroom in the basement of our boarding house. We do pretty good work. I've developed a few for Ab from time to time. Mostly we do it for friends for fun."

"Would you do these?" She patted the case. She hated to obligate him. Maybe she should ask Sid if he just wanted her to ship the film to him.

"If you want me to."

"I'll ask my boss first." She hopped out. Standing on the curb, she said, "Please let me know if I can go back over tomorrow."

"I'll let you know." He tipped his hat and was gone.

At the front desk of the hotel she checked for messages and wasn't surprised to learn that Shel had called several times. How was she going to keep him at bay while she wrote up the stories?

More than that, how was she going to write up the stories and not incriminate the women she'd interviewed? Maybe Sid would consider a full story in the rotogravure section in a Sunday edition. They could let the photos tell the story. But then Sid was expecting feature stories in addition to photographs.

Her room was stifling hot. She called the desk and asked for an oscillating fan to be brought up. After it arrived, she plugged it in and placed it on the floor next to the desk where she was orking. She began to pound out the story as fast as she could ype. She'd telegraph the skeleton of the information and post he stories in the morning's mail. Sid would be proud of her.

Midway through her work the phone rang. It was Shel.

"Hey, hey, Baby. Where have you been hiding? I looked all ver town for you this morning."

"Not in all the right places evidently."

"Where were you? I wanted to take you to lunch. But it's still ot too late. Want to have lunch with me?"

"I can't. I'm a working girl. Remember?"

"What about tonight? There's a swell moving picture show-ng at the Rialto, then we can go to dinner later."

She really had no plans for that evening. "Tell you what. Let ne get my work done this afternoon and I'll go with you this vening."

"Great. And then tomorrow I want to take you around and how you what great work they're doing at all the aid and sup-ly stations."

"What about the hospitals? Will you take me to the hospitals oo?"

He hedged. "Don't think I can do that. They're heavily guarded."

"Why? Are the wounded going to attack someone?"

"Hey, what's that supposed to mean? Surely you understand he ramifications of this thing, Clarette. They still don't know who's responsible for these atrocities. Many of those colored nen who are in the hospital will have to appear in court. They've been charged with inciting a riot. As long as they're under sus-icion they must be guarded."

She chided herself for the rude remark. No matter how she was feeling about all this, she needed to stay as neutral as pos-ible. A reporter hears all sides. But she couldn't help wonder-ng if there were any white men under suspicion. "I'm sure you're right," she told him, "but I bet you could get me in."

"I'll see what I can do. See you tonight at seven."

"See you, Shel."

For the rest of the afternoon she kept the typewriter clacking away. Simply putting together the news stories wasn't enough. She needed to write it all down—all her feelings, her reactions, her emotions. She wanted to vividly describe the destruction lest it fly out the windows of her mind and she lose it forever. It all seemed so senseless. The killing, the destruction. She wanted to know the why of it all. Why would men form a mob, then loot and torch the homes of other people? It made no sense. The quiet expressions on the faces of the women she'd met made no sense either.

She leaned back in her chair and read over the pages she'd written. There were way too many for a newspaper article. A magazine article? Could be. It was a thought anyway. After all, she didn't owe her soul to Sid and the *American*. She slipped the pages into a large brown envelope and placed it in the bottom drawer of the bureau. A glance at her watch told her the afternoon was quickly getting away.

She freshened her face and headed for the train depot to telegraph the information to Sid. She could send it from the hotel, but the station seemed the wiser choice. A railroad employee might not be as embroiled in the matters of the city.

Since it was between trains, the station was nearly empty. The station manager was a wizened old man with wisps of white hair sticking out from under his green visor. He tugged at his black half-sleeves as he looked over the material she handed to him.

"You sending all this?" he asked around a wad of tobacco in his cheek.

"All that."

He nodded as he pulled his biscuit watch from his vest pocket, then glanced at the white-faced wall clock. He did it almost without thinking. Clarette realized his entire life must center around trains arriving and departing on time. "Will you be waiting for a reply?" he asked.

Clarette thought a minute. *No sense in waiting*. It would take a while for Sid to receive this and review it. "If there's an answer, I'm at the Hotel Tulsa," she told him as she wrote her name and room number on a note pad. "Just have it delivered."

He spat in a brass spittoon at his feet, making it ding. "We'll do it, ma'am." She paid him and left.

On the way back to the hotel she scanned the department store windows. There were a number of classy shops in this town. Displayed in the window of Renberg's was a mauve silk dress which was distinctively Vanderpool. Suddenly she was jerked back into reality. It was as though from the moment she'd arrived in Tulsa she'd forgotten who she really was. Few people here would know or care what the Vanderpool name stood for. *A refreshing thought*.

Thinking about home, she wondered if her father might read her stories. If he did, he would see that all stories were not canned, and that free press was still a reality.

At seven she answered the knock on her door. There stood Shel dressed in a furry raccoon coat and plunking on a ukelele. "Do boopy do! Boogie woogie be bop," he said in a singsong voice. "How do you like my get-up?"

She had to laugh at the sight of him bundled up in a heavy coat on a steamy hot summer evening. "You big buffoon! What are you doing?" She ushered him in and closed the door.

"Trying to show my out-of-town guest a good time." He strummed the ukelele and sang a few bars of "I'm Forever Blowing Bubbles." After strumming a few more bars, he said, "I wish we were having another dance tonight." He grabbed her and twirled her around a couple of times. "How about it? Let's go to my house and we'll turn on the Vic and just have a dancing good time all by ourselves."

"I think not." She gave him a playful shove. "You promised a good moving picture, remember? Now you'd better get out of that coat before you have a heat stroke."

"You're right." Pulling it off, he slung it on the upholstered settee, and lay the ukelele down on top. "But you do like it?"

"It's a real wow! Leftovers from Princeton-Harvard games?"

"You bet. Rah rah rah, sis boom bah." He strolled over to the typewriter. Pushing down a key, he asked, "So, did you get your work all done?"

"All done." She grabbed her purse. Since there seemed to be bad blood between Shelby and Erik, she wasn't going to tell him about her visit to Greenwood that morning. He fished around with a few questions about her work, but she remained politely evasive without actually telling him to mind his own business.

Clarette hadn't been to a moving picture in weeks, and she was delighted with the show, a drama starring Mary Pickford. Afterward, they walked to a nearby restaurant where they talked about a wide array of subjects. Clarette could see that Shelby had a quick, bright mind. Had he not been spoiled with such ready wealth, he might be more motivated to make something of his life.

"Ever see a real oil well?" he asked as they finished their meal. "Silly question," he added quickly. "Being from New York you've probably never been close to one."

"You're right. No room in downtown Manhattan for an oil derrick among the skyscrapers."

"Let me take you down to the Glenn Pool area near Sapulpa. I'll show you one of Dad's leases. You'll be fascinated."

"Shel, I appreciate your kindness, but there's no time. I'll probably be leaving in a day or so."

"Oh yeah. Somehow I keep forgetting. It's as though you came flying into my life just for me." He reached out and covered her hand with his. "I know I'm being bold, but I've taken quite a fancy to you."

She drew her hand back. "I think we'd better go."

Outside, the air felt lighter than earlier in the day, the mugginess having been blown away by a slight breeze.

"Have you seen the refineries across the river?" he asked as they drove back down Main.

"I've not had time to see much of anything."

"You must see this," he said. "You can't leave Tulsa and not see this sight."

As he drove south of town, she recognized the area as the neighborhood where his house was located, but he passed the driveway of the Harland home. "There on the right," he said, pointing to a massive mansion on the top of a hill, "is the Patton place."

"Where the girl lives who. . ." As soon as she'd said it, she knew she'd slipped.

"Girl who what? What have you heard about Sadella?"

"I didn't know her name," she lied. "I just heard that the Patton girl is the one who accused two Negro boys of accosting her— or something to that effect." Hurriedly she added, "My chief in New York had a few sketchy details about it."

She was relieved that he seemed satisfied with this explanation. "I sure didn't know that story was out," he said. "I can't wait till this mess is all over with and forgotten."

"Maybe you could tell the story to me."

"Nothing much to tell. Two of them nigra boys attacked her in an alley in town. She identified them and they were taken to jail."

"Did she know them?"

He nodded. "One was the son of their cook, Chloe. I guess the other boy worked with their yard crew."

"If they knew she could easily recognize them, why would they risk their lives by attacking her? Seems a little odd."

"Clarette, you've obviously never been around nigras much. There's no explaining why they do what they do." He tapped his finger at his temple. "A little touched, you know. I've been around them all my life, and I can tell you."

As they crested the hill, the Arkansas River lay below. He drove down to the road that paralleled the river, pulled off to the side, and stopped the car. A billion stars spangled the expanse of sky. A bright moon spread shimmery ripples on the water. Across the way, the refineries, like sentries, lined the west bank. Some had fire dancing from the tops, burning off the gas. The golden flames joined the moon's reflection dancing in the water.

Shel jumped out and hurried around to open her door. He reached out his hand. "Let's walk a way." He reached out to put his arm around her shoulder as they walked along. For a time they walked in quiet, enjoying the night sounds. Presently, Shel pulled her to a stop. "Clarette," he said, "I know I've only known you a short time, but already I care deeply about you."

Taking her hand, he pressed her fingers to his lips. "You're a delightful lady. You're beautiful, intelligent, courageous, fun. . ."

"Whoa. Don't pour it on too thick." But she enjoyed the words. She was strangely flattered to think he'd been attracted to her so quickly. Before she could think of what he might say next, he was pulling her to him and kissing her warmly. At first, she didn't resist. It was a sweet, almost innocent kiss. But then she came to her senses.

"Please, Shel," she said pushing him away. "You're going much too fast for me."

"But you're leaving me soon. I have to move quickly."

She tugged at his hand. "I think you'd better take me back to the hotel."

# eleven

Clarette's senses were still spinning when she stopped at the front desk for her messages. The clerk handed her a telegram which meant Sid had sent his answer. She took the envelope and tucked it in her hand bag. She could read it after Shelby left.

"Thanks for a wonderful evening," she told him as they waited for the elevator. She couldn't understand why his kiss should have her in a befuddled state. She'd kissed other men and the kisses had been meaningless. All in fun.

He squeezed her hand. "*You* made it a wonderful evening."

At the room, she reminded him about his coat and the ukelele. "Oh yeah. Can't forget my college gear. I might need it next November when the New England snows blow in from the North Pole."

She chuckled at the remark. Secretly she hoped he would return to school so she could see him again. As she turned the key in the lock and opened the door, her smile disappeared. A shudder of apprehension coursed through her body.

In the middle of the sitting room floor lay her opened camera, the film bag lying nearby. The exposed film slides were gone. Her knuckles pressed against her lips to quiet a gasp of fear and shock.

Shelby pushed past her. "I was afraid this would happen," he said, surveying the room.

Clarette couldn't make herself move from the doorway. She leaned heavily against the frame. Panic squeezed her throat. Her feet didn't know whether to flee or stay. In the wire waste basket by the desk were two empty film canisters.

"My photos," she whispered. "Someone stole my photos."

Shelby strode into the bedroom and came back out again. "No one here. They're long gone."

"How could anyone get in?"

"Bribing a bell boy or a chambermaid would be the simplest way. Not too difficult."

"But why?"

"You tell me." The puppy-brown eyes weren't laughing now. "Where were you this morning? Why would someone want to destroy that film?"

She collapsed into the chair by the desk. "I went into the riot area and talked to a few of the women there. I took photos as well."

"How? There're guards everywhere. You don't even have a green card."

"A reporter from the *World* took me."

"That doesn't make any sense. They don't. . ."

"Oh, for heaven's sake, Shelby. It was a guy named Erik Torsten. His cousin is in Greenwood so he was taking things to her and I went along."

"Tessa. So that's where she went."

There was something about the way he said her name. She looked up at him. "You know her?"

"Barely. Many in town say she fueled the fire that set this riot into motion."

Clarette remembered that sweet innocent face and instantly knew no truth was in that rumor. "This town seems to thrive on rumors. I just wish I could find truth for once."

"I wish you'd told me about Torsten."

"Why?"

"He may have set you up to pull you out in the open."

That thought froze in her brain. "Oh, no. Erik?"

"I wouldn't put it past him. After all, he's pushing to become a big time reporter for the *World*. What better way to get a feather in his cap?"

*Shel could be right.* Clarette remembered how rude Erik had been to her when they first met. It was odd that his attitude had changed so quickly. But then, he hadn't invited her into Greenwood. It had all been *her* idea. Still, he might have used it to his advantage—sort of like a back-handed Hank Maxwell. Her mind struggled against the thought.

"Look around to see if anything else is missing," Shelby instructed her as he picked up the phone from the desk. "I'll call downstairs to get the police here."

"Should we?"

"What? Call the police?" He set the phone back down.

She nodded. She dreaded the publicity that would arise from this. It would prove she'd been snooping around where the city officials had told her not to go. She wasn't so sure that was the best idea. "Let me look around first."

In the bedroom she searched through her belongings. Her money was still stuffed under things in her drawer. Thankfully, the envelope filled with her other writings was there as well. From what she could tell, the film was all that the intruder was after. From the other room, Shel's solemn voice sounded. "Clarette, take a look at this."

He was standing by the desk looking at her typewriter. There was a sheet of paper in it. She never left paper in the new Underwood. "What is it?"

"Come see for yourself."

She willed her feet to cross the room. There was a message typed on the paper:

*Nosy yankee reporter go home! We don't need your kind in our city.*

She pulled the paper out of the platen. "I can't believe this. What kind of person. . . ?"

"Come and stay at my house tonight, Clarette. It'll be safer. My folks would love to have you. In fact, I think Dad rather likes you."

The offer was tempting, but Clarette thought better of it. That wasn't the answer to the problem. "Thank you, Shel, but I'll stay here. I can't run." Her initial fear was growing into anger. What made these people think they could treat her like this?

He picked up his coat and the ukelele. His funny entrance earlier in the evening seemed years ago. "If you insist. And you're sure you don't want the police to investigate?"

She shook her head.

"When I leave, take this chair and shove it under the doorknob."

"That's a good idea. Thanks."

He put his arm around her and gave a squeeze as he kissed her forehead. "I'm so sorry this had to happen. I hope you'll be more careful from now on."

"I will."

She did as he said by firming the straight-backed desk chair in place beneath the doorknob. *But that won't help when I am gone from the room.* Exhausted, she sat down on the bed. She'd never been threatened before in her life. What was it she'd said to her brother only a few days earlier about taking risks? She'd been so cocky when she said it.

Now what would she do? Her plan of action had seemed so clear. Just then, she remembered her telegram from Sid. Pulling it from her bag, she ripped it open and was hit by a new wave of shock:

FORTIER STOP OWNERS OF THE PAPER PULLING YOUR STORIES STOP THEY SAY "NO NIGGER STORIES" STOP COME BACK TO NY IMMEDIATELY STOP SID

At two in the morning, Clarette was pacing the small space

between the bed and the window. Sleep had fled. Her thoughts were racing like a runaway locomotive. Sights and sounds jumped around in her head—the burned-out city, the looted homes, the young mother nursing the baby who had been born in the midst of terror and destruction. Mama Sue had said the girl had not yet learned if her husband had survived the riot. Didn't they deserve to have their story told? Tessa, who'd been shot because she dared to befriend the Negroes. And Chloe who'd lost her son to the hangman's noose. Who would tell their side?

She thought of Erik and his decision to betray her. Why would he do such a thing? He didn't seem that type. Of course she didn't know for sure that he was the one, but who else knew she had been in Greenwood?

She stood at the window, cupping her elbows in her hands, staring at the straight row of street lamps running down Third Street. Maybe it was the guard whom Erik had spoken to. He could have followed them and spied on her. For that matter it could have been the manager at the train depot who had telegraphed her message to Sid. He may have leaked the information. In a town this size—a town that had recently experienced such a terrifying upheaval—it could have been anyone.

But now her boss was telling her to drop everything and come home. Could she do that? Every rational part of her mind said, of course she could. She had to. This horrible event didn't concern her. She'd been sent to get a story, and now the higher powers at *American* didn't want her story. It was as simple as that. Perhaps her father was correct in his opinions of today's journalists and newspapers.

But in spite of everything, she had to protect her job. If she continued her work as a newspaper reporter, she would eventually see dozens of stories like the Tulsa riot, and meet dozens of people like Chloe, and Tessa, and Mama Sue. *You'd better get used to it, Fortier,* she chided herself. *You can't get mush-brains over every little incident.*

That being settled, she kicked off her slippers and lay back down on the bed. First thing in the morning, she'd call the train depot for departure times. Then she would pack.

ぉ

It was barely five when there came a light tapping at her door. At first she thought she was dreaming. When it came a second time, fear froze her. What if it was the ones who'd broken in and stolen her film? Still groggy from lack of sleep, she pulled on her robe and slippers and made her way into the sitting room. She heard a girl's voice.

"Miss Fortier? Are you there?"

"Who is it?"

"It's me, Tessa Jurgen."

Relieved, Clarette moved the chair from the door and opened it. There stood Tessa wearing the same homemade dress. Her hair was now down and fastened at the nape of her neck, the golden curls hanging down her back. In her hand was a simple summer straw hat.

"I'm so sorry to bother you at such an early hour, but I thought fewer people would see me at this time of day. This city seems to stay awake through the night hours and sleep in the mornings."

Clarette smiled. "Come on in." She motioned Tessa to the tufted settee, as she switched on the fringed lamp, then pulled up the desk chair to be closer to her. "I wish I had some refreshment to offer you. It's not exactly home sweet home."

Tessa smiled. "I'll only stay a minute. I wanted to thank you for what you're doing here. We feel God directed your steps to us."

Where had Clarette heard that phrase before? *Shades of Grandmother Vanderpool.*

"I know of no other out-of-town reporter," Tessa went on, "who has cared enough to ask the people of Greenwood about what happened. No one wants to hear their side."

"I gathered that."

"As Mama Sue said, there should have been no guns. There were mistakes made on both sides. But the mindless burning and looting was cruel and heartless."

Clarette agreed. She kept silent and allowed Tessa to talk.

"I was afraid after what Mama Sue said about the Klan you might get frightened and leave. I wanted to assure you that the strict guarding will lessen within a few days. The martial law lasted only a short time, the presence of the National Guard lasted only a short time, and this American Legion citizen's guard will be the same way. They make a show of being tough, and then it's over." She gave a slight smile as she rubbed at her wounded arm. "They can be scary, but as Mama Sue said, they're nothing compared to the power of God."

"You believe the guards will be relieved of their duties?"

She nodded. "And soon. Those are working men. They can't stay away from their jobs forever. I'd give it another day or so and you'll be able to go in and out of Greenwood with no trouble at all. You won't even need to rely on Erik's green card."

That was a nice thought, but Clarette had to remind herself she wouldn't even be in Tulsa in a day or so.

"I've heard they're beginning to release the men and boys in the internment centers as well," Tessa added.

"Really?" Now this interested Clarette.

"On Sunday, Preacher Sam's going to hold church service outdoors near the church, then they're going to gather at Preacher's and Mama Sue's back yard for a meal. What better place for you to interview people who went through the experience. They'll be gathered together in one spot. You won't have to go chasing all over looking for them."

It sounded perfect. Just what she needed. Too bad it had come too late. She didn't have the heart to tell the girl she was being forced to drop it all and leave. Perhaps she could just tell Erik and have him relay the message to her later today. Let Tessa keep her dream a few more hours.

How odd that Tessa seemed to think *God* had sent Clarette here. If that was true, God wasn't doing a very good job of keeping her here. If God cared about anything at all on this earth, the riot wouldn't have occurred in the first place.

"I appreciate your remarks and your help," Clarette told her. "By the way, what does your fiancé think about your involvement in all this?" She remembered Erik saying he was close friends with her fiancé.

Tessa's cheeks colored and her blue eyes glowed. "Gaven's right by my side. At first he couldn't understand my feelings, but the Lord changed his heart." She gave a little shrug. "It was a miracle."

Clarette had her doubts about that. "And what about your cousin?"

"Erik? I sought him out the moment I learned Jasper was in jail and begged him to help, but he refused. Of course, looking back, I'm not sure he could have done much. The headlines in both papers were already stirring up the white citizens to take the law into their own hands. But after Jasper was killed so brutally, Erik had a real struggle realizing he hadn't even tried to help. I think that's why he's been coming over trying to help now. He knows the Lord's forgiven him, but now he wants to do as much as he can to make things right."

Tessa rose to go. "Thanks again, Clarette. Maybe we'll see you later this morning when Erik comes over."

"Maybe you will." As Clarette closed the door behind her departing guest, she whispered, "And then again, maybe you won't."

Clarette returned to her bedroom and watched out the window as Tessa climbed into a red roadster where a waiting driver whisked her away. *Her fiancé Gaven, no doubt.*

For a moment she stood gazing at the city as the first rosy

tints of dawn began to color the sky. It was hard to believe that only a few short years ago, this had been an out-of-the-way cow town and before that, an Indian village, on the banks of the Arkansas.

On occasions, she'd seen an Indian or two walking along the Tulsa streets in their blankets and leather leggings. Near First and Main, she'd seen an Indian store which featured feathered headdresses, beaded moccasins, and handmade Indian jewelry in the window, a witness of days gone by. Then the oil boom swept through and changed everything. How she would delight to browse in that Indian store and ask questions. What a great magazine story that would make. In fact, there seemed to be a million stories in this miniature city.

She turned from the window. *A million stories.* Why hadn't she thought of it before? She was sitting right in the lap of stories that other editors would pay dearly for. If the *New York American* didn't want to hear what she had to say, maybe she should look for other outlets.

She fished around in the bureau drawer for her envelope and pulled out her writings and looked them over once again. She could stay in Tulsa while she finished writing about the riot and support herself by selling other articles. If Sid fired her, she could always find another job. Suddenly her heart was racing as the new plan formed solidly in her mind.

# twelve

From her handbag on the bureau, she pulled out a black leather address book as she tried desperately to remember the name of a fellow with whom she'd gone to college. Romney something or other. He'd sat next to her in her senior journalism class. She'd heard that he was now on staff at *Mosaics Magazine*. Surely the freethinking spirit of *Mosaics* would want to hear what she had to say.

She flipped pages until finally she found the name under the K's. *Of course, Kimball. Romney Kimball.* She recalled what a serious guy he had been, and how he had talked incessantly about freedom of the press.

But first she would have to call Sid. The clock on the table by the bed proclaimed it was nearly six. That meant seven in New York. Maybe Sid would be in his office.

His booming voice sounded on the line the moment Central put the call through. Thankfully the static was lower today. "Miss Fortier," he said when he realized it was her on the other end, "I trust you have your ticket and are headed back to New York pronto."

"Sid, why wouldn't you print my stories?"

"Now kid, that telegram wasn't written in Chinese. The money that owns this place wouldn't give the nod. They don't like it. If they don't like it, I don't print it. It's as simple as that."

"But what about truth? What about free press?"

He gave a groan. "You sound like you still have pigtails and a skip rope. Time to grow up. This is how things are. Now get yourself back here. We've got ample supply of stories in the Big Apple for you to cover. Hey, I hear McDow's court date is ming up. I'll let you have that. How's that?"

"I'm staying here, Sid."

"You're what? What are you, nuts or something?"

"I'm not nuts. There are stories here, and I'm going to write em and have them published."

"That's mighty big talk."

"Maybe."

"If that's what you want, you understand I have no choice but give you the boot."

"I know." Clarette felt a cold shiver run up her back. Was she ut of her mind? This was the job she had wanted so desper- tely only a short year ago. But if they were afraid to print the uth. . .

"Okay, kid. There're plenty of others in this city who would ive a right arm for your spot. It won't be empty long."

She knew that was true. "I'll take my chances here."

"Tell you what I'm gonna do. I'll give you the rest of today to hange your mind. At midnight your job is gone. Poof. Van- hed. Got it?"

"I understand. And thanks."

Through the crackling on the line she heard him add. "You re got more spit and vinegar than I gave you credit for." Then ere was a click.

The gruff old man wasn't so bad after all, once you got past e crusty veneer.

By the time she dressed and put on a dab of lip rouge, it was ate enough to call Romney at *Mosaics*. To her delight, he re- embered her. She explained the situation as briefly yet as early as she could, winding up with the fact that the *New York merican* wouldn't print what she was reporting.

"You're calling us at the perfect time," he told her. "We were iscussing racial unrest just the other morning in an editorial eeting. It was stated we needed more inside information. I ever have felt the press was giving the whole story about what happened out there. We found the same was true in Omaha."

Clarette felt her heart beating faster.

"What about photographs? Will you have photographs?"

She paused. All her film had been stolen—but she could get more. "Yes," she assured him. "I have my camera and I'm a pretty good photographer."

"Great. How soon can you get the first installment to us?"

"Installment?"

"Yeah. We could do this in weekly segments. With each segment, let's add in a side story about one particular person."

She thought of the young mother with the new baby. Or maybe even Chloe. "There're plenty of stories here. I'll have the first installment in the mail to you early next week."

"Terrific. I'm so glad you remembered I am at *Mosaics* Clarette. This is going to make me look good with my boss."

He sounded as though she was doing him a favor. But there was still one more matter. "Can you wire me an advance?" she asked. "I have no job now, and my expense money is nearly used up."

"I'll ask the boss and let you know." He paused. "I can probably talk him into it."

"Thanks, Romney. I'll be in touch."

Hanging up the phone, she was amazed at how easy that had been. Finding a place to live would be her next project. Perhaps she could slip away into a new residence and the culprits who had written the note and stolen her film would think she'd gone back to New York. But where? And how could she locate it? When she went downstairs for breakfast, she would purchase a newspaper and scan the ads. Anyway, she was dying for a cup of coffee.

As she started to leave the room, the phone rang. She was surprised to hear Erik's voice. His was a quiet voice. A gentle voice.

"You up?" he asked.

"I'm up."

"I'll be taking a few more things over to Tessa and the others this morning early. I won't stay long." She waited a moment as he seemed to be collecting his thoughts. "I didn't know if . . . Do you want to go back?"

Now she wasn't sure what she should do first. She needed more film. She wanted to call a few more editors to see who might be interested in her other stories—*National Geographics* was now a consideration. She also needed to quickly find a less expensive place to stay. "Tessa told me the guards might be taken off duty in a day or so," she said.

"Tessa? You've talked to her?"

"She stopped by here at about five this morning."

"That gal gets around. What did she want?"

"Just to thank me I guess."

"Sounds like her. But what's the point about the guards?"

"Then I can come and go freely. Without your green card."

"Oh." Did she detect a note of disappointment? Surely it was her imagination. "Well, even if you don't need my card, you still need a way to get around. I don't think Harland is going to take you in there. And no cabs are getting through."

He was right. "Are you offering your services?" she asked.

"I am. That is, if you want to keep investigating the stories. I can also take your film with me today and develop it for you tonight."

The mention of the film quickly brought back the scare she'd had last evening. She'd better not tell him about that. "I think I've found another place to develop the photos for me. Thank you anyway for offering."

"But I was going to do it for you at no cost." He must have seen through her bluff as quickly as she'd decided to produce it. "Did something happen to your film, Clarette? I thought you knew how to use a camera."

What was the use? The guy was hopeless. "Erik, someone

broke into my hotel room last night and stole all my exposed film."

His voice tightened. "Were you hurt?"

"I wasn't here."

"Out with Harland?"

"Mm-hm. We went to a movie and dinner."

Erik was quiet. "I'll be right over." Then he added, "May I come to your room?"

*What a gentleman.* "You may," she told him.

Within twenty minutes, Erik was sitting where his cousin had sat only two hours earlier. He asked her about each and every detail of the theft. She told him all she knew. When she showed him the threatening letter, his face reflected concern.

"This is typical of their scare tactics," he said when she was finished. "Now what? I guess you'll be going back to New York."

In spite of what Shel had said about Erik, his openness seemed to belie any clandestine motives. His face was transparent almost to the point of being embarrassing. "Do you think I should go back?" she asked.

"Should?" He ran his fingers through his blond waves. "Yeah, I suppose it'd be much safer if you did." He pointed to the threatening letter. "They mean what they say, you know."

"But what do you think? About me going back?"

His smile softened his features. "I was sorta hoping you'd stay a while longer."

Clarette would have liked to have flattered herself into thinking he wanted her to stay because of personal reasons. But of course that wasn't it.

"You're the one God sent to tell these stories," he said. "At this time, you seem to be their only answer. The colored folks, I mean. And I'd like to stand ready to help as much as I can."

*Appeasing his guilty conscience no doubt.* "Well, for your information, I just this morning relinquished my job in New York in order to stay on here."

The blue eyes widened in surprise. "You did what?"

"You heard me." She rose and went to the bedroom to retrieve the telegram from Sid. Handing it to Erik, she said, "This was my ultimatum. I learned this just after I discovered the break-in last night."

He studied the message, then said, "A double blow. I'm so sorry." His voice was velvet soft. She wasn't quite sure how to handle this kind of response. "And after this you told your chief you were staying here?"

She nodded. "Under the circumstances, he had no choice but to fire me. I've already called the editor of a New York magazine and have a go-ahead from them to write the stories in weekly segments."

"What magazine?"

"*Mosaics.*"

"I've read it. A good magazine. They seem to be pretty fair." Somehow Erik didn't seem the type to read *Mosaics.* But then, what type was he? She barely knew him.

"And now you're staying after all." He hooked his foot over one knee and leaned back in the settee. "I guess you'll need a place to stay."

Did this blond Swede have a crystal ball? He was better than the fortune tellers at Coney Island. "Precisely. I was starting to go down to breakfast and study the ads in this morning's paper when you called."

"Tomorrow's Saturday. I can take you around to look. Are you thinking about a boardinghouse?"

"I'd prefer an apartment."

He nodded. "I know of a couple nice ones over on Frisco Street." He grabbed his hat from where he'd tossed it on the table. "I'll go get you a couple boxes of film. It'd be best if you not be seen buying any more film for a while."

"I can't slink around and hide."

"No, but you can use God-given wisdom and be careful."

He stood. "I'll be back in a few minutes and we'll have break
fast. You going with me back over to Greenwood?"

"I'll go."

The blue eyes glittered. "I thought so."

≈

By ten that morning, she had fresh new film, new photos, and
notebook full of added information from the ladies at Mam
Sue's. At Erik's suggestion, she gave the exposed slides over t
him. "No one can steal what you don't have," he told her. "Gave
and I can work on these tonight. I'll have them for you tomor
row so you can pick out the best ones and have them ready t
send in next week."

She was grateful and told him so. As they parked back at th
hotel she asked him, "Do you know any Indians?"

"Indians? Don't tell me you're going tourist on me."

"Not hardly. I just thought a couple feature stories about lo
cal Indians would help right now. I considered asking at tha
Indian store on Third Street, but stories work much better i
you have a good contact."

He nodded. "I know a few Indian families up north of the cit
in the Osage Hills."

"Could you introduce me? Or set up an interview for me?"

"If you were any other reporter from New York, I'd turn yo
down cold."

"But since you promised to help in any way. . ."

"I did say that, didn't I? Sometimes my mouth gets me in th
craziest messes." But then he grinned, and the light that wen
on in his eyes sent a shiver through her. "Sure. I'll run you up t
the Osage hills. How about Sunday afternoon after church?"

*Church. Who said anything about church?* She kept forget
ting this man was religious. She found it hard to imagine as sh
considered his towering physique. The broad hands double
into fists could probably put a man in the hospital. She couldn'
envision them folded in prayer.

"Tessa said," he went on, "that she'd invited you to attend the Mount Zion services on Sunday."

"Oh dear, I nearly forgot. She suggested it as a way to corner several interviews at once."

"I could pick you up at Mama Sue's after dinner."

She nodded as she stepped out of his Model T. "It's a deal."

At the hotel desk, there were several messages from Shelby. She hurried to her room and called him.

"Where've you been?" he demanded. "I've tried all morning to call you. Surely you didn't go back over to Greenwood. Not after what happened last night."

She paused a moment, trying to think up a lie to tell him. But her pause answered his question.

"Clarette, what am I going to do with you? You don't seem to realize the Klan doesn't play games. You could be in grave danger."

The serious tone in the voice of the fun-loving Shelby sobered her. Had she made the wrong decision to stay?

# thirteen

Shelby wanted to come over right away and "talk sense into her." But she couldn't let him barge in on her writing time. She had to begin the first installment for *Mosaics.* After much discussion, they decided Shelby would come to pick her up at two.

When he arrived, he was still vehement about her staying out of Greenwood and away from the Negroes. "I've offered to take you a number of places where I know you'll be safe, and you insist on jumping into the most dangerous hot spots." He shook his head. "I don't understand."

She looked at his young handsome face as he stood inside the door of her suite. Shelby was a wonderfully likeable fellow. In fact, she liked him as much or more than any man she'd ever been with, and his concern touched her deeply. "I'm sorry to worry you, Shel," she told him gently. "I know I can't make you understand, but it's ingrained into the heart of a reporter to nose out the news. Rather like a bloodhound on the scent."

She stepped closer to him and allowed him to envelope her in his arms. "Sure," he said. "Like a bloodhound. Trouble is, you may have bloodhounds after you." He tipped her chin up and kissed her lightly. "Look, I twisted a few arms and obtained permission to get you into Booker T. Washington School today, in addition to visiting the relief aid stations. Now what more could you ask?"

"Why a school?"

"They've converted it into a hospital."

She gave him a squeeze. "You mean it? I can talk to the Negro patients there?"

He laughed. "Sure. But only one or two. Now didn't I tell

you I'd help you? I wish you'd trust me."

"I never said I didn't trust you."

"Your trip back into the riot area shows you don't trust me."

She pulled away from him. "Shelby, I've been fired from the *New York American*."

"Fired? Why? What'd you do?"

"It's not what I did. More like what I didn't do. My boss ordered me back to New York, and I refused to go. I'm going to write for other publications and stay around for a while."

He reached out for her arm and drew her back to him. "Clarette, I'm thrilled. I was dreading the moment you'd have to leave. Now you can come to the Harland house and stay. We have plenty of room. You won't have to worry about rent or anything." His warm kisses made it hard for her to think. "I'm so glad you're staying in Tulsa," he whispered. "Now we'd better get going. We've several stops to make."

As they drove to the makeshift hospital, Clarette considered his invitation. It seemed to be the perfect answer, and yet she cringed at giving up her independence. She wouldn't give him an answer until she'd looked at the apartments of which Erik had spoken.

❧

The visit to the hospital was distressing. She was limited to one small area and allowed to talk to only two men. Past them she could see row after row of beds. It was hard to guess how many wounded were there. A guard informed her that a first aid station and dispensary were also available in another part of the building. When she asked to see it, Shelby said she'd better not.

During the interview with the patients, Shelby was by her side, as well as a doctor and two nurses standing nearby. Their presence hindered the process. Both of the wounded men were noncommittal and she detected fear in their eyes. Spending her time at Mama Sue's was much more profitable.

From the school, they drove to several aid stations located at various white schools and churches. At each location, a few women were sorting and labeling clothing and bedding. The efforts, it seemed to Clarette, were minimal in light of the vast needs.

By the time they visited the last location, the afternoon was far spent. With all due respect to Shelby's noble efforts, she felt the time had been a waste. But she couldn't make him understand.

As they drove back to the hotel, he invited her to go out on the town with him that evening, but she had to refuse. "If I'm going to freelance," she said, "I'll have to spend time writing."

The sad puppy eyes reflected his disappointment as he stopped to let her out at the hotel. "I feel like I have you back, and now I want to be with you every moment," he told her. "Tell you what, let's gather your things, check you out of the hotel, and you come to my house tonight. I'll call Mother from the hotel and tell her to prepare an upstairs room for you. A room overlooking the rose garden." He reached for her hand. "I promise I'll leave you alone and allow you to write. It would be enough for me just to know you are safe—and close by me." His sweet smile was infectious.

"Thanks, Shel, but give me a few days. I need time to think about this. I can't rush into it."

Reluctantly, he agreed.

"I tell you want I need from you, though."

Shel instantly brightened. "Anything. Anything at all."

"I'd like to do a few articles about the oil boom."

"Say no more. I know all about that. My offer to take you to Dad's leases still stands. I'll show you where our first gusher came in. I can give you all the vivid details you'd ever want to have. We can run over there tomorrow. Or how about Sunday?"

Clarette winced inwardly. Tomorrow she would be looking at apartments, and Sunday she would be in Greenwood in the morning, and with Erik in the afternoon. "I'll be tied up with stories all weekend," she hedged "But how about Monday?"

"Monday it is." His disappointment had dissipated.

&#x27 b

That evening she called Herta to ask her to package a few items and send them to her. Her roommate was aghast. "How will I pay all the rent with you gone?" she asked.

"It'll just be a few weeks, Herta," she explained. "June's rent is paid, so don't worry. I'll send you money for the parcel post and for this call." She went over a list of what she needed and Herta read it back to her. Although Clarette wanted to tell her friend all that was happening, the static prevented her from continuing the conversation. "I'll write you soon and let you know all the details. Thanks for your help."

"Hurry home. It's kind of lonely without you," Herta said as they rang off.

Clarette considered the remark. She felt rather happy to be missed.

&#x27 b

Erik came by Saturday morning and drove her to several apartment houses. All were sufficient, but the rent prices were higher than she'd expected. Erik explained it was because of the influx of oil company employees. "The landlords are going to get whatever they can," he said. Which made sense.

She did agree to look at a boarding house, but the room was rather small, and she dreaded the thought of eating with others who might be snooping in her business. She needed the privacy of an apartment. Perhaps she should agree to go to the Harlands' after all.

Just as she was about to give up, Erik thought of one more place. "It's out of the city," he said, "but the trolley runs out that way."

"I'm used to being outside the city," she assured him.

"It's near the Lincoln school on Peoria. An old widow lady named Mrs. Effie Halleck rents out the back part of her house.

I don't know why I didn't think of her before. She's real particular, but she knows me. One of my old girlfriends from college used to live there."

Even though Clarette didn't comment, his face reddened at the mention of this old flame. "The place may be rented. We'll have to pray for a miracle."

Amazingly enough, Erik's prayer was answered. The house was a modest bungalow with double gables and a broad front porch. The apartment was perfect, and at a rate she felt she could afford for a few weeks.

Following the death of her husband, Mrs. Halleck had had the house remodeled to create an apartment in the back half of the house.

It featured the existing kitchen and bedroom, plus a newly created bath. The door connecting the front to the back of the house had been sealed off, creating a totally private dwelling. The kitchen meant Clarette could eat there as well. The furniture wasn't new by any stretch of the imagination, but it was certainly adequate. The back door opened into a quiet yard where flowers were struggling to grow in the intense heat.

The gnarled old lady was hopelessly deaf and never seemed to catch where her new renter was from, nor what her occupation was. But Clarette didn't care. It was better that way. After the threatening note, she'd just as soon lie low for a while. She secured the place with a deposit, saying she'd move in on Monday.

As they drove back toward the city, Erik showed her the trolley route. "And Swan Lake is only a few blocks away. I'll take you there one evening if you'd like. We could rent a row boat and take a ride across the lake."

"Sounds nice," she told him. And it did. "Thank you so much for helping me find the apartment."

He gave a wave of his broad hand. "Think nothing of it. Glad to be of help. By the way, I've asked Gaven and Tessa to come to the hotel to pick you up in the morning and take you over to the Mount Zion church. Or what's left of it, I mean." His blue eyes turned to her. "Is that all right?"

"If it's all right with them."

"Oh, it is. They wanted to be there with Chloe and the others for the first service after. . ." He groped for the words. "After all the destruction."

"You won't be there?"

He shook his head.

"Tell me how Tessa came to be so close to these people."

"I'm not sure. As Tessa told you, she worked as a tutor and nanny for the younger Patton children, and Chloe is the cook there. The two struck up a close friendship and the Patton family didn't like it."

"Why?" But even as she asked it, she knew. She remembered the persecution Herta talked about during the war simply because her family was German. Prejudice was everywhere.

"Mrs. Patton's from a Southern family who owned slaves in the past. That may have something to do with her feelings for the Negroes."

"So they ordered Tessa to discontinue the friendship, and she refused. Is that how it happened?"

He pursed his lips and nodded. "Courageous little gal. She told me she'd rather die with them than to betray them. And she almost did." The last few words were in a whisper.

His compassion stirred something inside Clarette.

"I love Tessa as though she were my own sister. I don't know what I would have done if something had happened to her. Especially after I turned my back when she cried out for help."

Back at the hotel, she thanked Erik once more for all his time and help. He again insisted it was nothing. "Gaven and Tessa will be by at ten in the morning, then I'll be at Mama Sue's at about one to pick you up. See you then."

❧

As they drove through Greenwood the next morning, Gaven explained to her a few more details about the night of the riot. Clarette immediately liked Gaven. He had a wide bright smile, and seemed intent on clinging to his tiny fiancée. Their wedding date was set for next spring. Gaven, she learned, was a grade school teacher who clerked in a grocery store during the summer.

The American Legion guards had been relieved at midnight Saturday night, just as Tessa had predicted. Gaven parked his roadster, and as they were getting out, a heavyset man walked toward them, his ebony face shining beneath a panama hat. "I say now. This here must be that New York City lady I's been hearing about."

"Clarette," Tessa said, "this is Preacher Sam. Preacher Sam, meet Miss Clarette Fortier."

The man tipped his hat to reveal wooly white hair as he offered a warm smile of welcome. "I's so glad you is here. Mama Sue done told me all about you and your writing. We're much obliged you want to tell all the story." He wiped sweat from his hat band with a handkerchief before replacing the hat. "You know you gonna get flak 'cause of this, don't you? You ready for that?"

"It's already started," she told him. "If I'm not ready, it's too late."

He gave a chuckle which rumbled up from his broad midsection. "God loves that spirit in you, child. Yes, He do. Like little David slinging rocks at Goliath."

Clarette had no answer for his remarks, but he didn't seem to notice. "Come on over here, folks. We's getting ready to start the service."

Folding chairs were set out in rows in a cleared area next to the ruins of Mount Zion Church. Brightly colored quilts scattered about served as the church pews where clusters of families were beginning to congregate. Tessa was also correct

that a number of the men had been released from the internment centers on Saturday. Many men had gathered with their
wives for the service.

Clarette felt hot unbidden tears burning in her eyes as she
spied the young mother who had been at Mama Sue's with her
baby. Sitting close beside her on a quilt was the young man
who was obviously her husband. Thank goodness he was safe.

They were welcomed by Mama Sue and Chloe and others
who kept thanking Clarette for coming. She hoped they weren't
putting too much stock in what she was doing. After all, she
could fail.

Clarette followed Tessa and Gaven to the hard, wooden folding chairs close to where a makeshift podium had been erected.
The hot sun shone down relentlessly. Preacher Sam stepped up
on the podium and addressed the group.

"Now I's gonna preach today with my hat on," he told them.
"I know I ain't s'posed to have no hat on in church, but the
Good Lord understands I need a little shade today." He gazed
skyward as he said it, and the crowd murmured their agree-
ment.

Mama Sue joined him to lead the song service as the group
belted out hymns loud enough to rock all of Tulsa. Clarette had
never heard hymns sung like this. They stood to their feet and
clapped out the rhythm. They swayed with the beat and sang
from the depths of their hearts in perfect harmony. They were
without organ, piano, or hymnbooks, but none were needed.

Clarette was amazed that they could sing in the presence of
the massive destruction about them. Presently Mama Sue
stepped down and Preacher Sam began to preach.

Clarette had never heard his kind of preaching either. Shouts
of "Amen," and "Praise the Lord," from the congregation ac-
companied his message. At one point he told them, "None of
them folk who died here. . ." and he waved a hand to take in the
blocks and blocks of burned and looted buildings, "ever thought

they was gonna draw they last breath this soon. But they died
and went out into eternity. Was they ready? We don't know. But
is you ready?" He paused to wipe the sweat from his brow with
his handkerchief. "You can be ready to walk on streets of gold
with sweet Jesus. Just ask Him into your heart today."

Later, she couldn't recall much of what Preacher Sam had
said, but she couldn't forget how it had made her feel. Like the
hot sun had all of a sudden moved from out of the sky and
begun burning inside her chest.

# fourteen

ater at the dinner, Clarette busied herself by moving among
ie people and asking as many questions as she could, filling
er notebook, and trying to block Preacher Sam's words from
er mind.

How this dinner had been put together was a mystery. Boards,
laced across saw horses and covered with tablecloths, held
owls, kettles, and pans full of a variety of foods with marvel-
us aromas. One of the ladies commented that her garden had
een trampled, but she'd found a few good tomatoes.

The men here were more willing to talk than the ones in the
ospital at the school. By piecing together what she'd learned,
ie realized that an organized opposition existed in the com-
iunity. Most likely the Klan activities had brought it into exist-
nce, out of self-defense. The lynching of Jasper Franklin had
een simply the last straw in a number of whippings, beatings,
nd lynchings of various blacks in the community. The men
ad felt they could take it no longer. But never had they dreamed
iat taking a stand would be so costly.

Already she heard talk of plans to rebuild as soon as possible.
hey would need housing by fall in order to be protected from
ie cold winter winds. It would be a mammoth undertaking.

By the time Erik's Model T pulled up, enough material filled
er notebooks to cover several segments.

Clarette had brought along her trousers and middy to change
ito for their trip that afternoon. While she fetched her change
f clothes from Gaven's roadster and went to change, she heard
fama Sue insisting that Erik come and eat a bite with them.

When Clarette came out the back door of Mama Sue's house,

he was chatting with Gaven. He was hatless and the sun made his blond curls glow. Dressed in his shirtsleeves with the cuffs turned back, he stood with his arms folded and his legs apart as they chatted amiably. Gaven's smaller stature served to accentuate Erik's broad shoulders and long legs. When he saw her, he offered a welcome smile and a wave.

Within minutes, they were in the Model T traveling north out of Tulsa on a well-worn dirt road. Chugholes and ruts from earlier spring rains gave the road the effect of driving over an old washboard. Erik's strong hands worked hard to keep the automobile in the tracks. She had to keep reminding herself that she'd asked for this.

In a little over an hour they arrived at the townsite of Okesa, which, Erik explained, was another oil boom town. The town was nothing more than a widened stretch of the dirt road with a few wooden buildings on each side. Scattered about the businesses, in no particular order, were other carelessly thrown together shelters. A mixture of horse-drawn wagons and automobiles were parked here and there. The most prominent buildings seemed to be the saloons.

They drove through the town, then turned off the main road and drove a mile or two across the prairie on what was nothing more than a wagon trail. The landscape soon changed into tree-covered hills. The motor of the Model T strained at the inclines.

"My friend, Grayhorse, is an Osage," Erik explained to her. "A few years ago, his land was leased by a Tulsa oil company. My father has helped the Osage tribal members get good prices for their leases. Otherwise they'd be taken advantage of."

"Is your father an attorney?"

"No. Just a very fair-minded businessman who cares greatly about Indian welfare."

She looked at him with interest. *Another story.* She was right. This place was filled with great stories. "Will this Indian, Grayhorse, want to talk to me?"

Erik nodded. "I called and asked his permission first. I think he likes the idea of being in a magazine."

As they came over a ridge, spread out in a shallow tree-filled valley before them was the Osage village. The village was a strange mixture of rounded Indian lodges, white-framed farm houses, and a smattering of small barns and outbuildings. Teams of gray-brown mules, hitched to wagons, flicked their long ears and switched ropy tails. Other mules and horses stood about in a split log corral. Outside the entrances of each lodge were stacks of kindling. A few dogs greeted them as they approached, excitedly jumping and barking. Indian women milled about dressed in traditional Indian garb with blankets draped over their shoulders. One had her baby strapped to her back. Clarette hoped she could get photos as well.

Grayhorse came out of a trim two-story farm house. He wore a white western hat with a rounded top, fine white leather breeches with fringes down the sides, fully beaded moccasins, and a brightly colored blanket fastened at his waist. His black braids, neatly plaited, lay over his sturdy shoulders.

"Welcome, Erik Torsten," he said as he approached them. "It has been many days since you have visited the Osage."

"Sorry, Grayhorse. I've just been mighty busy."

"And this is the fine lady you have told me about?" His dark eyes twinkled in the bronzed face.

Clarette was treated to the sight of Erik blushing as he made the introductions. Grayhorse led them inside the house and into the parlor. The house was as modern as any she'd seen, with a Victrola, an upright piano, and soft rugs. She was, admittedly, somewhat disappointed that Grayhorse didn't live in one of the lodges outside.

Grayhorse did not remove his hat, but sat rather stiffly in a wing-back chair while pointing her and Erik to a horsehair sofa. His wife came into the room with a tray upon which sat a tall whiskey bottle and glasses. Grayhorse gave a slight smile and raised his hand. "Not for these visitors, Hannah. Just water." He looked at Erik, and Erik nodded.

Obviously, Erik was known to Grayhorse as a man who did not take to strong drink. Clarette found that interesting. Before Hannah left the room, however, she filled a small glass for Grayhorse.

"Your father is well?" Grayhorse asked Erik.

"You've probably seen him since I have," Erik told him. "I've not been home in months."

"The elder Torsten has been a fine help to the Osage."

Hannah brought the tray in again, this time with glasses of water. Clarette smiled at the young woman and received a shy smile in return.

Clarette had her pencils and pad out and began asking Grayhorse questions about how the oil boom had affected his life and that of the other Osage.

He waved his hand around to indicate the house and furnishings. "You see part. I can buy an automobile if I want. I am thinking about it. The land we have given up, in return we have things." He took a swallow of the whiskey from the glass. "The value of headright much sought after by the white men."

Clarette was puzzled. "Headright?"

Erik broke in to explain how the heirs of those with Indian blood are the ones who can inherit monies from oil leases. "But there are also 'guardians' horning in on the money. The guardians are usually white men appointed by the government to curtail the wild spending of the Osage. They can inherit money just as though they were of Indian blood."

"Headrights are of value to white man, as scalps were to Indians in days past," Grayhorse added wryly. He turned to Erik. "Two more unexplained deaths in past two weeks."

"This passes the headrights down to the guardians," Erik told her, as she furiously took notes. "Then the guardians are free to collect the oil money."

There seemed to be as much lawlessness in Osage County as there was in Tulsa. But here the motive seemed to be greed, while in Tulsa it was simply hate.

Later, following the interview, Grayhorse agreed to stand with Hannah outside one of the lodges so Clarette could take photographs. Both maintained stern, somber expressions. As she was busy with the photos, Erik walked over to the corral and stroked one of the sleek, well-bred horses. When she was finished, he called her over.

"I suppose being from New York City, you're a greenhorn with horses."

Clarette chewed her lip. She and Aubert had both spent their earliest years on horseback, put through rigorous training by their horse-loving father and their hired horse trainer.

"Actually I have ridden," she told him. "I have relatives in Jersey who have horses." It wasn't a lie.

"Want to take a quick ride? We won't go far."

It was an interesting thought. "I'd love to."

Erik turned to Grayhorse who had walked up behind them. "Do you mind if we ride?" Erik asked.

The dark eyes were twinkling once again. "Take the fine lady for a ride through the cool woodlands. The white man has not yet put oil wells by the rock spring."

Within minutes the horses were saddled with lightweight saddles not unlike the English saddle to which Clarette was accustomed. Erik took the lead as he guided his roan up into the hills behind the houses and away from the road. She followed on a mild-mannered buckskin mare.

The air was much cooler among the scrub oak. They didn't talk. It was enough to soak up the quiet of the countryside and listen for bird sounds above them. Squirrels chattered, rabbits scurried for cover, and a covey of quail flushed out, then fluttered only a short distance away. Presently, he pulled up and stopped. As she did the same, he pointed off into the distance where she saw a doe and a fawn standing together.

Clarette liked the Osage Hills. Tranquility filtered from the peaceful atmosphere and seeped through to her insides. She found herself watching Erik's muscles through his light-colored shirt as he masterfully rode up a trail through thick underbrush. Dappled light through the trees intermittently shone on his wavy blond hair. She admired Erik's quiet manner and inner strength. He didn't keep her laughing as Shel did, but he certainly made her think.

She wondered why he continued to assist her so willingly. It was clear from what Tessa said that he wanted her to get the stories about the riot because he felt guilty for abdicating his own involvement. But that wasn't true in this case. Why would he take the time to bring her here to the home of Grayhorse?

"Where are we going?" she asked presently.

He turned back to look at her. "You getting tired?"

"Not me. I could ride forever."

"We're going to the rock spring that Grayhorse talked about."

"Does that mean a drink?"

"Nice and cold. So cold you can hardly drink it."

"Sounds wonderful."

The spring was located beneath a rock ledge, nearly hidden by a tangle of underbrush. "We'll have to leave the horses here," Erik told her. They dismounted, and he took her hand and helped her up through the craggy rocks to where the water trickled out of the hillside and down into a gurgling stream. Pale green feathery ferns draped about the opening like curtains.

"We didn't bring cups," she said.

"Just use the one the Lord gave you." He knelt down by the edge and scooped a handful, slurping noisily which made her laugh.

At the sound of her laughter, he turned and flicked water up at her. She squealed as the icy water hit her. "Ooh, it's so cold. Wish I had a bathing suit." She knelt down beside him and scooped up her own handful. The cold felt wonderful on her dry throat.

"Take off your shoes and socks," he told her.

"I will if you will."

"You're on." He was already untying his brown shoes.

Clarette didn't have to roll up the legs of her knickers, as they were only knee length. Together they proceeded to walk bare-foot, hand-in-hand down the shallow stream bed. The rocks on the bottom were fine and soft. Small fish scurried away in front of them. Erik's hand felt strong and firm over hers.

"'For the invisible things of him from the creation of the world are clearly seen. . .'" he said.

"There you go again, sounding like my grandmother."

He looked down at her. "You're grandmother's a Christian?"

Clarette nodded. "She's always spouting those tricky little phrases."

"What's tricky about them?"

"They never make much sense."

"I just quoted from Romans the first chapter, and it makes perfectly good sense. It quite clearly says that God is invisible, but his creation is not. I see God in all of creation."

He made it sound so simplistic, but of course it wasn't. She'd discussed religion with her friends at school for hours, and of one thing she was certain—no one really knew the truth about the Bible for sure.

When she didn't answer, he moved to safer subjects. "What do you think of Oklahoma now, Clarette?" he asked.

"I like it more each day," she replied with all honesty. "It's wild and free and rugged."

"There're a lot of problems here too."

"There are problems everywhere."

"I suppose so."

The water pooled deeper at a curve farther down the hillside. It was now up to her shins. Seeing something sparkling down in the water, she released his hand to step over to investigate. "What could it be?" she asked.

"Probably a crystal of some sort."

As she moved, she stepped on a flat stone that was slippery with moss and felt herself falling, but Erik's arms were immediately around her. "You'd better watch your step," he said, placing his large hand at her waist and pulling her to him. His words were a warm whisper on her cheek. Before she could answer, his lips came down ever so gently on hers.

# fifteen

Clarette was shocked, not so much at his kiss, but at her own eagerness to respond. She touched his face and inhaled his sweet warmth. Secretly, she'd been wondering what it would be like to have those strong arms around her, and the reality was more wonderful than she'd ever imagined.

Suddenly he drew back. "I—I'm sorry, Clarette. That wasn't fair of me. Here." He moved away from her to fish about in the water for the stone she'd been seeking. It was a lovely piece of clear quartz. She put it safely in the pocket of her trousers.

Silently, they walked back up the stream bed to the rock overhang. He helped her out and lifted her up onto the wide flat rock, then took a seat beside her.

"Clarette, there's something I need to tell you."

"About what?"

"About me." His voice was low and serious.

"You sound like it's something terrible."

"It could be."

She couldn't imagine anything bad being connected to Erik. He epitomized good.

"Remember when you asked me where I was the night of the riot?"

"I remember. You said you were out of the city."

"Right. I want you to know the whole truth. As I told you, Tessa had come to me and begged me to stand with her against voices in the city that wanted to hang Jasper Franklin and his friend Strapper. By the way, the reason Ab doesn't want anyone seeing the files is because a few of those issues were highly inflammatory—calling for vigilante action."

Clarette had assumed as much. She let him continue.

"After the crowd had stormed the courthouse and gotten the boys out. . ."

"The guards at the jail just gave them over?"

"When you face a mob like that, there's not much choice. Anyway, I hung back, and later that night I heard that Strapper had broken away and miraculously escaped. Since they were happy to have one to lynch, they didn't chase him, planning to get the bloodhounds out after him the next day."

He slid down off the rock, picked up her shoes and socks and handed them to her as he put his own back on. "As soon as I heard, I knew it was up to me to find the boy and get him out of the state."

"You?" She sucked in her breath. "What a dangerous mission. How'd he know you weren't trying to capture him?"

"I took an old Osage scout, by the name of Night Storm, with me. Stormy knew exactly how to follow his trail and find him fast."

"He must have been terrified."

"He was glad to see us. Strapper's name fits him. The kid is almost as big as me. Other than being exhausted, he was amazingly peaceful. He loves the Lord and was ready for whatever happened."

That statement made no sense at all to Clarette, but she didn't dare pursue it.

"Big as he was, we made him curl up on the floor in the back and covered him with blankets. It was a warm night, too. I drove the old Model T fast as I dared straight to the state line."

"What if the mob had found you?"

"Like as not I wouldn't be sitting here talking to you. But as Tessa said to me, it wasn't any worse that what went on in the war. I did what I felt needed doing."

"What happened to the boy?"

"I let him and Stormy off in the Ozark hills. Stormy stayed

with him for a few days, showing him how to get around in the hills. We're in the process of trying to get a higher court to hear the case. Meanwhile, if this were known, I could be prosecuted in Tulsa county for aiding and abetting a criminal."

"Criminal." She scoffed at the word as she pulled her knee socks back on.

"Anyway," he said, "I thought you should know. Come on, we'd better get back to town before dark."

❧

That night, as Clarette lay staring at the light streaming in through her hotel window, the rich, full-throated voices of the folks at Preacher Sam's church echoed over and over in her mind. Vibrant voices, singing powerful hymns, full of hope in spite of the death and destruction surrounding them.

She had never believed in a heaven or hell. She agreed with her college friends that when you died, you died. That's all there was to it. Even her professors believed that.

Grandmother Vanderpool had said that God would guide her steps, then Tessa and Erik both stated that God had sent her here. And now, she had decided to stay. Of course that was merely a coincidence, but it was kind of a spooky coincidence. She was staying because she believed that truth should be reported, not because some vague God had anything to do with it.

But stranger than all that was Erik's kiss that afternoon in the shady grove with the cold water swirling around their ankles. A more romantic spot, she couldn't imagine. But why had he kissed her? And why did he feel he needed to tell her about his involvement in the escape of the boy named Strapper? What if she decided to turn him in? Of course she wouldn't, but how could he be sure she wouldn't?

She sat up in bed, propped her elbows on her knees, and pushed her short hair off her forehead. As wonderful as it had been to be swept into his strong arms, she certainly never wanted to be involved with a man who was so religious. Erik Torsten could hardly speak one sentence without spouting some Bible verse. It was exasperating and kept her always on the offensive. She didn't need that kind of problem.

Shelby was the one she took greater pleasure in. His humor and lightheartedness was pure joy. She was excited about going with him in the morning to the oil fields at the Glenn Pool. In fact, she'd call him first thing in the morning and ask him to come and help her move her things over to her new apartment.

She recalled how excited he'd become when he'd learned edshe wasn't returning to New York. Shelby made no secret of how much he wanted to be with her. Thinking about Shelby made her forget about the scary words of Preacher Sam about dying and heaven and hell. She then flopped back down on her pillow and was quickly asleep.

**⋙**

Shelby was more than willing to help her move her few things into the new apartment. He was at the hotel early—early for Shel, that is. She had her bags all packed.

When he stepped in her door, he pulled her into his arms. "Have I told you how thrilled I am that you're staying? And I'm glad you found a place," he told her between the light kisses he planted on her nose and cheek, "but I still wish you were staying with us."

"I know, and I appreciate your thoughtfulness, but this is best."

As he drove out Fifteenth Street toward her new home, she found she was relieved to be getting out of the hotel, especially after the break-in. Her new place would be more secluded and private.

"So how did you find an apartment clear out here?" he asked as he followed her directions.

"I just started looking around." She never knew how much to tell Shel about Erik, nor how much to tell Erik about Shel. It was quite confusing. It was obvious they didn't care for one another.

But when Mrs. Halleck came around to greet them as they were taking in the bags, the landlady pointed a wrinkled finger at Shelby. "This ain't the big tall Swede feller what brought you here the first time. How many men friends you got, gal? I don't mean to put up with no nonsense around here. This here's a respectable neighborhood."

Shelby looked at Clarette. She shrugged and tried to mask her sheepish expression. She should have known she couldn't keep it quiet.

"Torsten?" he mouthed at her. She nodded.

"There won't be any nonsense," she told her new landlady.

"What was that again?" Mrs. Halleck asked, cupping her hand behind her ear.

Clarette repeated it three times, each time louder than the last. By the time she'd said it the third time, Shelby was giggling.    "I'm not sure your landlady believes you," he said to her as they started out toward the Glenn Pool. "After all, here you come around with two different men. . ." He shook his head as he guided the Kissel out over the bridge spanning the muddy Arkansas River. "I don't see why you'd want to spend time with that big ape-man anyway."

"Shel, please. It's a free country. I can be with whom I please. When Erik learned I wasn't leaving the city, he remembered this apartment he knew of. He drove me out to see it and it was available. That's all there is to it."

He reached over and patted her arm. "I hope so."

To change the subject she began asking him questions about his father's work in the oil business. And he was more than pleased to tell the story of how his father was one of the earliest wildcatters to make a strike in the area. But the elder Harland was also one who stayed in the business by buying up multiples of neighboring leases.

"I was with Dad the night the first well blew in. Crazieest thing you ever saw. Dad's partner saw signs of oil on the bit and started shouting loud enough to wake the dead. Dad and I came to watch. They put the bit down again and we could hear the sound of the oil starting to gurgle and chuckle and surge. Suddenly there it was, shooting clear up over the derrick. That was the beginning. Now I've lost track of all the leases we have."

"I guess that brought big changes in your life."

"You could say that. The years before the strike, we lived in a tumbledown shotgun shack and barely had enough to eat. I never want to live like that again."

"Have you ever worked on the rigs with your father?"

He wrinkled up his nose. "Not me. An oil lease is a rough, rowdy, dirty, stinking place. Dangerous too. Fires, tornadoes, drunk roustabouts shooting one another. No thanks, I don't want any part of it."

"What is it you'd like to do with your life?"

Shel grinned and shrugged. "I'm not sure. But I have plenty of time to figure that out. I'm still young."

She turned him back to the oil stories and jotted notes as he shared them. Later, he said, "Tessa Jurgen is from this area."

"The Glenn Pool?"

"Yeah. She was a teacher at a school out here."

"That little thing teaches school?"

"At country schools you can do that with only a certificate from the county superintendent. Then she hired on as a tutor for the Pattons."

"She's so young." Clarette couldn't imagine the girl teaching school where some of the kids were probably twice her size. After a moment she said, "You care about her, don't you."

Shel looked over at her. "Why do you say that?"

"I don't know. It's how you say her name, I think."

"It doesn't matter. She's totally inaccessible—I couldn't beat Mr. MacIntyre's time. Besides, she's much too religious for my blood."

*Now that remark sounded strangely familiar.*

The oil lease Shel took her to was almost as fascinating as the Osage Indian village she had visited with Erik. A forest of derricks rising to the sky stretched out across the landscape, interspersed with fat, round storage tanks. Hundreds of trees had been felled to build derricks and storage tanks. The creek bank was void of foliage because of fires and the overflowing of crude oil. Shel showed her where they were in the process of converting wooden derricks and tanks to more substantial steel structures.

As Shel had said, it was a dirty place. The oil field workers were grimy, looking as though they wouldn't come clean with a week of scrubbing. Getting close as she dared to the pounding, pumping rig, she talked to workers and took photos.

Once she had enough material gathered, she and Shel drove to Sapulpa where they had lunch at a small restaurant. While they ate, he told her stories of his father, like the time Elmore had taken a crew into a farmer's field to drill. The farmer didn't own mineral rights, but only surface rights to the land. Of course, he would have been paid for damages to his crops, but he wasn't going to allow that oil crew in. The farmer stood guard at his gate with a shotgun in hand.

"My dad had been following the freight wagon in his car. He told the wagon master to get down—that he would drive the rig past the gun-toting farmer. But that farmer was intent on having his way. He came up to the wagon and poked the gun right in Dad's ribs."

"But didn't shoot?"

"Thank goodness he didn't. And at that point, Dad turned around and went back. It wasn't until they had an official Indian agent with them that they were able to get that particular well spudded in." He gave a shrug. "See what I mean? Maybe I was born into the wrong family. I would never have that kind of tenacity."

Clarette almost felt sorry for him. It was as though he kept measuring himself against the accomplishments of his father and always came up short.

As they drove back to Tulsa, she said to him, "Surely there's something you must dream of doing, Shel."

"What would it matter if I did? The Harland name is oil, oil, oil. I don't fit in oil, so I don't fit."

"So leave town, change your name, and make it on your own."

Shel turned to her so quick, he almost went off the road. "You make it sound as though a person could really do that."

For a moment, Clarette considered telling him the truth about her family, but then thought better of it. The timing wasn't right. "People can do anything they set their minds to do," she told him. "This is a big country. You don't have to be what your father is. You can be anything you dream of being."

"Well, there is something I want to do. Promise you won't laugh."

"I won't laugh."

"Dad calls it pure foolishness."

"Your dad isn't the final authority on everything, Shel."

"In my world he is."

"So change your world. Now what's your dream? Tell me."

"Music," he said softly. "I write tunes, melodies. Music plays in my head all the time."

"Well, that makes sense. You're always singing. Music's a wonderful talent, Shel. A needed talent. Everyone loves music."

He was quiet for a time as the landscape whipped past them. "I've never had anyone tell me that before."

"Get a few of your songs scored, then plan to spend a week or so in New York and take them to every music company in the city. Then don't give up until you break through. It's the only way."

Suddenly, he pulled the speedster off the road into the shallow bar ditch, took her in his arms, and kissed her soundly.

You are the most wonderful girl I've ever met, Clarette. You've given my dreams back to me again. Thank you. I'm going to do exactly what you've suggested."

As usual, she had to talk Shel out of a supper engagement. "The evening will be spent writing," she told him. "Why don't you spend the evening getting your songs ready?"

"I think I'll do just that," he said. His enthusiasm was bubbling up. "Would you come over in a few days and give a listen? I want to know what you think."

"It's a deal."

By nine-thirty that evening Clarette had three articles ready to go. One was the first installment for *Mosaics Magazine*. She then quickly typed out a short letter to Grandmother Vanderpool, explaining a few of the developments in her life.

She'd just stopped to fix a cup of coffee when there was a light tap at her door. She opened to see Erik's tall form looming in the shadow of her porch.

He gave a slight grin. "I have your photos. I was working late in the newsroom, but thought I'd drop them off before I went home."

"Thanks, Erik. Perfect timing. I have the story ready to mail tomorrow."

She reached out to take the extended envelope from his hand, but he yanked it back. "The payment is to go rowing with me on Swan Lake."

# sixteen

She laughed at his subtle proposition. "And you told me this was for free," she teased. "Isn't it terribly late for rowing in the park?"

"This city doesn't come to life until after dark. The park won't close until midnight." He handed her the envelope. "Your photos are great, Clarette. You're really good."

She opened the flap and pulled out the stack. On top was a close-up of the burned-out house where the iron bedstead protruded up out of the rubble. He was right, they were all high quality. "Your developing skills are nothing to be scoffed at either," she said.

"It's a good partnership. Now what about the park? I'm offering a sincere invitation." He put up his hands. "No strings attached."

She thought a moment. She was dead tired. Her arms and shoulders ached from the hours of banging away at the Underwood. She tried to remember all the reasons she didn't want to be with Erik again—all his Bible-spouting, scripture-reciting ways.

He leaned against the porch post and smiled at her, the blue eyes crinkling. "I'll wait out here till you get freshened up and ready."

"I'll only be a moment." As she touched up her lip rouge and ran the brush through her hair she tried to explain to herself why her heart was thudding clear up in her throat.

At the last moment, she decided to shed her sailcloth skirt and take one of her sheer silks from the wardrobe. She surveyed her reflection with satisfaction as she pulled on the cloche to match. *Perfect.*

"I have some good news," he told her as they drove toward the park. "Word came back today that young Strapper is in Canada."

Clarette felt herself give a little sigh of relief. She'd been concerned about the boy ever since she'd learned of his escape from the lynching mob. "That is good news. How did he get all the way to Canada?"

"Sort of like a modern version of the underground railroad— one connection after another."

"I know that eases your mind. Especially since you risked your life to get him out of Oklahoma."

"He and his friend Jasper were both good students and hard workers. At least Strapper has a chance now."

The park was a gay affair with roller coaster and carousel—a tiny version of Coney Island without the beach. Erik took her hand as they strolled through the park toward the lake. There he purchased the ticket for a boat. He helped steady her balance as she carefully stepped from the wooden dock into the waiting row boat. His muscular arms rowed them away from the noisy crowds, glaring lights, and bouncing music.

Clarette stared up at the sprinkling of pin point stars flung across the sky. Neither of them spoke; the rhythmic plashing of the oars breaking the water intoxicated her. She felt drowsy and contented. Draping her arm over the edge, she let her fingers trail through the cool water. How had she let him talk her into this? She'd be much smarter to stay far away from this big, blond Swede. But she couldn't deny there was something special about him.

"Thank you for agreeing to come with me," he said at length, his husky voice breaking into the quiet.

"Thank you for inviting me. I needed the break."

"You look even more beautiful in the moonlight than in a shady brook on a secluded hillside."

Clarette felt her face warming. "You're very kind."

"But I'm not just being kind. I mean every word."

"Erik," she said, attempting to re-route the conversation, "in Preacher Sam's sermon yesterday, he talked like there's a literal heaven and hell. Do you believe that?"

He nodded. "Yes I do. Don't you?"

"Hell is just what you make it here on earth." At least that was what all her friends had said. "No one can really know what happens when a person dies. Theologians have been disputing it for years." She wanted to corner him. To break the flimsy bubble he seemed to carry with him.

"You can know, Clarette," he said with quiet authority. "You never have to wonder. In the book of John, Jesus says He's preparing a mansion for us in heaven. He said if it weren't so He would have told us. In First John it says the Bible is written so we can *know* we have eternal life."

He lifted the oars from the water and hooked them inside the boat, letting it drift aimlessly for a time. "Would God promise heaven, then not show us how to attain it, or let us know *if* we had attained it? That wouldn't make any sense."

"You're asking me? I don't understand much of anything about the God you're referring to." She was disgusted at herself for even having brought it up. It was as though she had to remind herself of their stark differences. As though she needed cold water in her face to break this spell he was able to weave over her. "You may think you like me, Erik, but we're worlds apart. I'm nothing like your cute little saintly cousin Tessa."

"I've never asked you. . ."

"It's quite clear how much you admire her. But I'm not like that, Erik. I'm a party girl, not a church girl. I'm just not your type. Now put the oars back in the water. I think I'd better be getting back."

The drive back to her house was in silence. She ached because she felt she'd hurt him. But things were better this way.

etter that he be scared off now before she fell hopelessly in
ove with this gentle giant.

As he walked with her to the back of the house, she felt she
eeded to give him one last clincher. "There's something else
ou need to know about me, Erik," she said, stepping up on the
orch step.

"What is it?"

"My name isn't Fortier. What I mean is, it's a family name,
ut it's not really my name." She was fumbling for words. She
as waiting for a questioning look from him. Perhaps a sur-
rised look, but the quiet, clear eyes were steady.

"I'm Clarette Vanderpool. My father is the head of the mas-
ve Vanderpool silk industry. He's worth millions."

Erik moved closer to her. "I'm the child of the Creator of the
niverse and my Father owns the cattle on a thousand hills."

"Now what's that supposed to mean?" But her words were
mothered in his gentle kiss.

"Erik." She pushed him away. "You're not even listening to
e. I'm trying to show you how different we are."

"A name doesn't make a person, Clarette. You're your own
erson. That's pretty clear. I'm glad you wanted to tell me the
uth. I want to know all about you, but that will have to wait
ntil another time. It's late and I've kept you far too long. Thanks
gain for agreeing to go. I had a wonderful time."

He kissed her again, and this time she didn't pull away.

"The Lord is talking to you, Clarette," he whispered into her
air. "And I'm praying that you have the ears to hear His voice."

With that he was gone, and she was left standing there weak
nd breathless. Once inside, she went to the bureau and rum-
aaged around for the New Testament that Grandmother
'anderpool had given to her. She found the scriptures he had
nentioned—but so what? How could she know if the Bible
vas really true or not? Then she noticed the red ribbon at the
ixteenth chapter of Proverbs. There was the verse from her

grandmother: "A man's heart deviseth his way: but the Lord directeth his steps."

Here she was living in Tulsa, Oklahoma, fired from her job in New York, and doing things she'd never dreamed of doing. The verse suddenly seemed strangely real to her. She shoved the Bible back in the drawer and slammed it shut. Hard! Atop the bureau lay the gleaming quartz picked up the day Erik had kissed her. She opened the drawer once more, tossed the quartz in beside the Bible, and slammed the drawer one more time.

The next morning she took the trolley into town to post her articles. As she went about her business, she was fighting a war inside her mind. It was frightening to think that Erik was praying for her. He probably had Tessa praying too. That was even scarier. Then she remembered that Grandmother Vanderpool in her mansion on Fifth Avenue was praying as well. It was enough to make a person sick!

❧

Within a couple of weeks, Clarette's articles were appearing in a number of New York publications. She was ecstatic. This was as good or better than headlines in the *New York American*. When the first installment appeared in *Mosaic Magazine*, she received a long distance call from her father. He'd seen the article! He was saying the words she'd waited a lifetime to hear.

"I'm proud of you, Clarette," he said. "I have a copy of *Mosaics* right here on my desk. Your article is well written. Packs a tremendous wallop. How'd you happen to write for the magazine?"

Briefly she told him the story of how the owners of the *American* had refused to print her story. She even told him about her apartment and her decision to stay on until the stories of the destruction of Greenwood were fully told.

"It was quite a blow when your mother and I learned you'd left my birthday party without even a good-bye."

"There just wasn't time. I'm sorry. I asked Grandmother to

convey my apologies."

"Of course she did, but it wasn't quite the same."

"You might not have been so amiable about my going as you are now that you've seen what I can do," she said in defense.

He paused. "Perhaps you're right."

Clarette wanted to ask what Mother and Aubert thought about her article, but she saw no sense in pushing the matter. This call was enough.

Again he told her how proud he was of her. She felt her heart warming down to her toes. She thanked him for his call.

"When your work there is done, will you be coming home again?" he asked.

It seemed a strange question since she hadn't actually been "home" for so many years. But as she pondered his question, she realized how unsure she was of her future plans. She rather liked being where she was. "I'm just not sure," she told him. "But I'll stay in touch."

"Please do," he answered before he rang off.

Clarette had to shake herself to be sure she wasn't dreaming. Her world seemed to right itself in that moment. But that wasn't all. The next day a call came from Sid.

"I wouldn't have believed it if I hadn't seen it with my own eyes," he said. "I gotta hand it to you, Miss Fortier. You're some dame."

"You saw my article?"

"Sure we saw it. It's been passed around the newsroom a jillion times. Just a minute, just a minute. Somebody else here wants to talk to you."

"Hey, Fortier." It was Hank Maxwell himself.

"Hello, Hank. Are you busy covering the McDow trial?"

"Most boring thing I ever sat in on."

"Serves you right. I'll never forgive you for taking my story."

Max laughed. "Looks like you didn't need it. I just wanted to let you know you cost me a ten spot."

"Sounds like an office bet."

"Yeah. I bet you'd never make it. I lost. *Mosaics* is some magazine." This was probably as close to a compliment as she'd ever receive from someone like Hank, but it was enough. "See you, kid. Here's Sid."

"Bye, Hank."

Sid's voice was back on the line, and she could see the cigar flipping back and forth in his mouth. "You probably got a few people mad as hornets at you by now."

"A few." She couldn't deny it.

"Just be careful. When they see you ain't quitting, they'll be even madder. Watch who you get friendly with."

"Thanks, Sid. I'll watch. Thanks for calling."

As she hung up, she couldn't help but smile at his fatherly concern for her welfare. Sid was a nice guy, even though he did play yes-man to moneyed people.

❧

Tessa had now moved out of Greenwood and was living with a girl named Pauline. Pauline and her family had an extra bedroom into which Tessa moved. From what Clarette had been told, most of Tessa's belongings had been destroyed in the riot. She and Gaven, however, continued to assist in the rebuilding of the area.

Clarette observed with growing interest as the population of Greenwood struggled to come back. It was now a tent city as the survivors attempted to create shelter before the autumn rains fell and the winter winds blew.

Through her insistent investigations, Clarette attempted to locate the graves of the ones who'd lost their lives in the conflict but to little avail. One little boy reported seeing a wagonload of Negroes' bodies being driven out of the city in the dark of the night. Others admitted they had been hired to dig the graves of their own people shortly after the riot had subsided. Her heart broke at the number of atrocities uncovered.

As July approached, Clarette realized she'd either have to send her share of the rent to Herta, or—a thought that was at once both frightening and appealing—tell her to find a new roommate and ship the rest of Clarette's belongings to Tulsa. Was she ready to cut that tie? She wasn't sure.

Shel hadn't been as much a pest since he'd become intent on getting his music ready to present to possible buyers back East. She spent a number of evenings with him in the music room at the Harland mansion. Although she knew little about music, her editing skills were of great value to him as they worked on lyrics. He was immensely grateful to her for all her help.

One evening they had enjoyed a highly productive time working on his songs. Clarette felt he possessed an immense amount of talent, and she believed he could make a go of it, if he would only apply himself. She told him so as he drove her home.

They were chatting amicably as he opened the car door and walked with her down the drive way and around the back of the bungalow to her door. Something lying on the porch made them both stop in their tracks. It was a bloodied copy of the *Mosaics Magazine* containing her article! Nearby lay the severed, bloodied head of a chicken.

## seventeen

Shelby grabbed her as she turned to bury her face in his ches Icy fear coursing through her made her tremble in the evenin heat.

"Stay here," he ordered.

"Don't, Shel. Don't let me go. I can't bear this. It's too aw ful."

"I've tried to warn you, Clarette, but you wouldn't listen. N one cares if you write about oil wells, but the Klan won't le you continue writing about the riot. They won't let you get awa with it."

"I didn't know it would be like this. How did they know wher I moved to?"

"It's a small town. I told you they don't play games. Nov stay here and let me take a look."

She watched as he cautiously moved to the side of the porc and peered in her window. "Doesn't look like anyone broke in. He crawled over the porch railing and studied the magazin lying there. Blood was splattered across the cover, and drops o blood were slung around the porch and down the walk. It was good thing Mrs. Halleck was deaf, or this could have fright ened the poor old lady half to death.

"I think this time we'd better call the police." Her voice wa scratchy.

"I'm afraid it might not do much good. People who do thing like this know how to buy the police department."

"Then what should I do?"

He looked over at her. "Just what I've told you from the be ginning. Stop writing about that infernal riot! Please, Clarette

Before something terrible happens."

Together they took pans of soapy water and scrubbed all the blood off the porch, again thankful that her landlady could hear little. As before, he begged her to come stay at his house for a few days for safety. As before she refused.

After he left, she couldn't stop trembling. At last she decided to call the *World*, taking a chance that Erik might still be there. She dared not disturb his boardinghouse where the phone was in the hallway.

A gruff voice answered the phone. She steeled her voice to keep out the trembling. "Erik Torsten, please."

"Torsten," the voice called out. "Some dame. Man oh man, I wish a dame would call me this time of night!"

Relief flooded through her as Erik's soft voice came on the line. "Clarette? Are you all right?"

"It's happened again. Another scare." Briefly she explained the scene on the porch.

"And Shelby Harland was with you?"

"We spent the evening at his house for a while. He brought me home and we discovered it."

"Rather a coincidence that he happened to be with you the last time as well."

"Erik, please. I know you don't like Shel, but that's not why I called you."

"Why *did* you call me?"

The question stopped her. "I—I'm not sure. I. . ."

"Don't answer that. I'll be there as soon as I can get away."

She mulled over his question as she put on a pot of coffee and waited for him to come. She was fearful of the answer—how much she wanted him there to comfort her, to say he would take care of her and protect her. As soon as he was at the door she was enfolded in his massive arms and crushed against his chest.

She showed him the magazine and places where she and

Shelby had scrubbed the blood stains off the porch. "What will you do now? Are you going to stop?"

"I'm not sure. Shel said not to call the police."

"He knows it wouldn't do any good. If I thought it would help, I'd print the whole story in the paper tomorrow. But Ab Schoggen is under the same influence as Chief Dwyer. Irrational action on our part now might cause more harm than the good you're doing with your stories. One thing is certain, you're hitting them where it hurts. You're speaking truth."

She invited him to come in and poured him a cup of coffee. He pulled a ladder-back chair up to the square wooden table. "Erik," she said, as she brought the cups over and sat down across from him, "for a fleeting moment this evening I grasped an image of the fear that the Negroes live with. It's such a sick, helpless feeling." She pushed the sugar bowl toward him and he shook his head. "I can't imagine living a lifetime with that fear. It must be awful. How do they bear it? I don't understand."

"'God hath not given us the spirit of fear. . .'"

"Oh please, Erik. Not now. Not more scripture. Can't you see I'm being serious?"

"I'm sorry," he said. "Sometimes I forget how natural it is to look to the Lord for help."

"Well, if you're such a great all-knowing, spiritual Christian," she said, "why do you hate Shelby Harland so much? Answer me that."

Erik leaned his elbows on the table and blew on his hot coffee, then took a sip before speaking. "First of all, I don't really hate him."

"Strong dislike?"

"Now hold on a minute. You asked and I'm trying to answer. It's not Shelby; it's the things he does, or doesn't do, that bother me." Slowly he traced a flower on the oil cloth with his forefinger. "Many of my good buddies from around here went to France with me to fight a nasty war. But Shelby and his ilk stayed home because of the favor purchased by family money. When you watch men getting blown apart, or dying slowly of the fever, you change. The unfairness of the system disturbs me."

Clarette cringed as she remembered how Aubert, while in the Army, had been kept in an office job because of the Vanderpool money. But she agreed with Erik. It wasn't fair.

"But I could overlook that. There were a few others with oil money who got to stay home. Shelby Harland is like a ship with no rudder, floating about life with no purpose or direction. He's easily swayed by those with the most power. He seems to be more fascinated with power than with hard work and diligence. Frankly, he scares me—he's like a little kid carrying a big gun."

"Purpose and direction are in his life now. He's working on a number of songs he's written. I think he can get them published."

"If you're there to push him, he might. But I guarantee you, the moment you stop, he'll stop. The momentum and initiative simply aren't there."

Clarette chose her words carefully. "Shelby suggested you might have squealed on me the first day you took me into Greenwood."

Erik looked at her with a steady, unflinching gaze. "But you didn't believe him, did you?"

It was more a statement than a question. "No," she admitted, "I didn't believe him."

"Why do you think he said it?"

"I'm not sure. I just thought it was because he didn't like you."

"Maybe it was because he was the informer," he said as he leaned back, balancing the wooden chair on the two back legs.

She shook her head. "Shelby may have his head in the clouds, but he's not ruthless." She fetched the pot from the stove and refilled their cups. "My editor in New York said something very interesting. He told me that in a race riot, you can never know who is on which side. That's truer than I could have ever imagined."

"Promise me something, Clarette. If you won't stop seeing Shelby, will you stop telling him all your business?"

She had been sharing a great deal with Shel lately. "I could do that."

"If I at least knew that, I'd sleep better at night."

She smiled. "Are you worried about me?"

The tipped chair came back down to the floor with a soft thud. "I think of you more than you'd care to know, Clarette Fortier Vanderpool."

A warmth rushed through her at the softness and gentleness of his words.

He stood to his feet. "I'll go now. Promise me you'll call me anytime—day or night."

"Even at the boardinghouse?"

"Even there."

She walked him to the door where he turned to place his hand at her back and leaned down to brush her lips with a feather kiss. "I'll be praying for your safety. God loves you, Clarette."

As he stepped down off the porch, she called out, "Erik?"

He paused to look back at her.

"Where's that found—that stuff about God not giving us the spirit of fear?"

He smiled. "First chapter of Second Timothy. Verse seven."

"Thanks."

"Anytime."

Before going to bed, she reviewed the third article in the series for *Mosaics*. The second installment would be published in a few days, and there was so much more to tell. Romney had discussed at least four or five more articles. Plus he liked the sound of an article regarding the Indians' danger due to the struggles over headrights. Writing was her livelihood, but could she keep on in face of these threats? *After all*, she thought as she put the envelope back into the drawer, *I could always pack up and go home.* She hadn't yet told Herta to find a new room-mate.

Then she almost laughed out loud. Who was she trying to kid? As the image of Erik's sweet smile made its way into the window of her mind, she knew she would be staying for a while yet.

She took the Bible from the drawer and looked in the table of contents for the book named Timothy. There was the verse just as he had said. But how could that be true? Everyone was afraid at some time or other. She, admittedly, was quite fearful now.

❧

A few days later, she carefully packaged her manuscript, along with the photos, to mail to Romney. When finished, she put the parcel down into her shopping bag and put a jacket on top. No need carrying such a conspicuous-looking package out in the open.

Even though it was barely eight-thirty in the morning, the Oklahoma sun was high and quite warm as she walked to the trolley stop near her home. She timed it so her wait in the hot sun would be short. Later, as the trolley made its way toward downtown, a hot wind whipped through the open windows. She was thankful the post office was a short three-block walk from where she disembarked. She firmed her broad-brimmed hat and adjusted the shopping bag as she stepped off onto the sidewalk.

Just as she stepped around the corner, two men dressed in white robes and hoods rushed toward her. There wasn't even time for the scream in her throat to be released before they grabbed her, clasped a hand over her mouth, and dragged her into a waiting car.

# eighteen

Clarette was shoved to the floor of the car as it sped away from the post office. One of the men stuffed a handkerchief into her mouth and said, "Now listen, sister, and listen good. We ain't gonna put up with no nigger lovers in Tulsa."

"What's in her bag?" came a voice from the front seat.

"One of them stories," said the hooded figure in the back seat. Her face was to the floor, but she could hear the sound of her story and photos being ripped to bits.

The car was driven not far outside the city, then screeched to a stop. She was roughly pulled up onto the seat. "My mama told me to always respect women," came the muffled words through the hood, "and I'm trying my best to be a good boy and mind my mama, but you're getting on my nerves real bad."

He opened the car door. "Let this be a fair warning to you, sister. Next time we won't be so easy on you." She was shoved out hard, and she hit the ground full force, rolling into a nearby ditch and taking in a mouthful of dust as she went. The wind was knocked from her lungs and she gasped to pull air back in. The remains of her story were thrown after her and floated to the ground as the car sped away.

She sat there trembling for a time before attempting to walk. Hot sun beat mercilessly on her bare head. Her hat had disappeared.

A few small farms dotted the horizon. After walking what seemed a long time, she came to a house and asked to use the phone. The lady was kind, but her eyes were wide with fear. Perhaps she'd seen the hooded figures in the car.

Clarette phoned the *World* office and asked for Erik.

"He's not here," came the answer.

"Not there? Where is he?"

"There was a shooting out at one of the oil fields. Chief sent m to cover it. He should be back late tonight. Any message?"

"No. No message."

She got Central back on the line and called Shelby. With help om the lady, she gave him directions and he was there within inutes.

In the car, Shelby could scarcely drive. He was trembling. Clarette," he said as he drove back toward town, "I'm going to ew York in a couple days." He turned to look at her. "Go with e. Go back with me, please. Get away from here, before some- ing very terrible happens."

"Shel, I'm all right." He seemed to be more shaken than she as.

He pulled the car off the road and stopped. He reached out r her hand. "Clarette, I never meant for it to happen like this. ow I've fallen in love with you. Oh, for heaven sake, please op all this nonsense. It's all so senseless. Go with me to New ork. Marry me and we can make New York our home. You can rite forever if that's what you want. What do you say?"

"You never meant for what to happen like what? What're you lking about? What's senseless? Helping people? Getting the uth published?"

He looked away. "When you first arrived. . ." His thin voice oke as he spoke. "I was assigned by the Klan to divert you."

"What?" She yanked her hand away. "Divert me? Shelby arland, you're lying. You can't mean it. You wouldn't."

He looked back at her, but she could hardly bear the pitiful xpression in his eyes. "I didn't know you then. I never planned fall in love with you. And I was so sure just a little note in the pewriter would shut you down."

"You're on *their* side?" Suddenly she was repulsed. "You say u didn't know me, but what does that matter? Why would you have done it to anyone whether you knew the person or not? Why would you enable those horrible people to get away with their diabolical schemes? I can't believe you would spy on me for them."

She felt like clawing his eyes out. So Erik had been right all along. "You left the coat and ukelele in my room, so they'd be sure it was the right room?"

He nodded slowly, tears forming in the puppy eyes.

"And you told them where my apartment is on Peoria? Then you made sure I was at your house so they could put the blood on the porch?" She sat there bewildered. "You probably arranged the visit to the hospital as well. What a phony!"

"I'm sorry, Clarette. I begged them to never hurt you. I was so sure you'd back off."

"Oh, you were sure, were you? Well, you're more wrong than you could have ever thought possible. Take me to Greenwood, Shelby. There's something I have to tend to."

He sucked in his breath and his eyes were filled with fear. "I can't, Clarette. I can't go over there. Don't ask me."

"Then take me close enough so I can walk. Now go!"

With limp acquiescence, he did as she asked. As soon as they were in the area, she knew exactly how to get to Mama Sue's house.

"Stop here," she ordered him.

"Clarette, please! I really do love you, and I'm begging you—don't go back in there."

She stepped out and closed the door. Through the window she said, "Shelby, do you know anything about God?"

"Some, I guess."

"Can you tell me how to know if I'm going to heaven or not?"

"Don't be silly, Clarette. This isn't the time for a theological discussion. You're still in a lot of danger."

"That, my dear Shelby, is precisely why I must find out."

Mama Sue's face lit up with a smile when she opened the back door at Clarette's knock. "Why, child, what you doin' in this part of town alone? Where's your big golden-haired angel you always with? Where's Mr. Erik?"

"He's out of town on assignment. Mama Sue, may I talk to you?"

"Course you can, child. I can tell you got somethin' on your mind." She opened the door wider and waved Clarette into the kitchen. "And your dress is tore. Somethin' done happened to you." Gently Mama Sue led her to the front room and sat her in the overstuffed arm chair, then brought her a glass of water.

After settling herself on the couch, Mama Sue said, "They finally done it. They roughed you up to put the scare into you, didn't they?"

Clarette drank the cool water and then nodded. "I was at the post office. They had on white hoods, just like I've always read about. They dragged me into the car. I was so frightened. . ."

Without warning, her body began to tremble and shake. The empty water glass became unsteady in her hand. "So frightened." The glass dropped from her fingers and clattered to the floor. She was on her knees by Mama Sue with her head in the black woman's ample lap, sobbing in deep gut-wrenching gasps.

"Now, now, child," she said, stroking Clarette gently. "Nothing wrong with being scared. We's all scared. That be the humanness of a person." She pulled a scented hankie from her pocket and pressed it into Clarette's trembling fingers. "Sweet Jesus watchin' out for you. Can't nobody take that away from you."

Clarette pressed the sweet-smelling hankie to her face and looked up at Mama Sue's open, giving expression. "But that's just it. I don't know that He's watching. I don't know anything. All I could think of was to ask God to spare me so I could know. Oh Mama Sue, if they'd killed me, what would have happened to me? I've got to know."

"You means to tell me a sweet, purty little gal like you ain't never ask Jesus into her heart?"

She shook her head. "I never believed there was a heaven or hell. I thought God was far away and impersonal."

"But you ain't never looked death in the face before, huh?"

"Never."

"It shore do make a difference. When you can almost peek over to the other side, you want real bad to know God is right there." She gave a deep chuckle that rumbled up from inside her. "Nice thing is, honey, you can know. Right now. All's you gotta do is invite Him in. He be standing there waiting for a long time."

"What if He won't have me? I'm not like Tessa Jurgen."

"You is you, Miss Clarette, and God love you just the way you is. But them bad things you be thinking about can fall away like cottonwood leaves after the first hard freeze. If you ask God to forgive your sins and use sweet Jesus' name, He do it. He say He will, and He don't know how to lie. Then when you is His child, you know you going to heaven the moment you die."

"Will you help me?"

"Be mighty happy to."

The prayer was simple and short. But after she prayed, Clarette knew she would never be the same again.

"The spirit part of you be new like a tiny new baby," Mama Sue told her. 'Old things pass away,' the Bible say, 'and all things is new.'"

Clarette blew her nose on the hankie. "Thank you, Mama Sue. Thank you for being here. Thank you for helping me find the truth."

"You got a Bible, child?"

Clarette thought of the Bible that her grandmother had so wisely presented to her. "I sure do."

"When you gets home, write down this day inside the cover. This is your birthday of being borned again. You don't never want to forget."

Clarette rose to her feet. "What a wonderful idea. I'll do it." She picked up the glass that had rolled a ways across the room. She handed the glass and the hankie back to Mama Sue. The dark hand took the glass, but pushed the hankie away.

"You keep that for your keepsake of this day."

"I will." She stuffed it into her dress pocket.

"I gots a hunch that big old Erik-boy gonna be mighty happy to hear your good news." Her eyes twinkled. "Now how's we gonna get you home?"

Clarette thought a minute. "How about Gaven and Tessa?"

"They'll be coming over when Mr. Gaven gets off at the grocery store."

"May I stay till then?"

"Honey," she patted Clarette's shoulder, "you always be welcome in this home. While we's waiting, we get out the Bible and I show you verses what will feed your hungry little soul."

❧

By the time Gaven and Tessa took her home, it was nearly six. Pint-sized Tessa had given Clarette a giant hug when Mama Sue had told them what had happened, and Gaven had shaken her hand and said, "Welcome to the family." Strange, but nice.

"Will you be all right?" Gaven asked as she stepped out of his roadster in front of her house.

"I'll be fine now. Thank you. Just. . ." It seemed odd to ask. "Just please be praying for me."

"That we can do," Tessa said with a smile.

Once inside she put in a call to the *World* to see if Erik was back. He wasn't, so she left a message for him to call. Then she did as Mama Sue said and penned the notation in the front of the Bible right beneath Grandfather Vanderpool's name.

As she scanned to find the scriptures that Mama Sue had given her, the shrill ring of the phone startled her. She hurried to grab it, expecting Erik's voice. It was Shelby.

"Clarette? Are you all right? I've been so worried about you all day."

"I've never been better, Shel. I found the answers I was looking for. I know now about God. I know that no matter what happens to me, I'll be with Jesus forever."

"Clarette, I'm calling to tell you to get out of town. Right now. Tonight. I can call and get the train tickets. You pack and I'll be over there to get you. If you have a trunk, my parents can ship it later. You're the one who suggested that I go to New York. You know the city better than I do. . ."

"I'm not going back to New York. I've got to get busy and rewrite the story they destroyed today."

"But that's sheer insanity. You have all the material you need to do the rest of the stories for *Mosaics*. There's nothing to keep you here now. You've got to leave!"

"The only sheer insanity I know of is your agreeing to work with such despicable people as those vigilantes in the Klan. Now that's insanity. What if I told you I like it here?"

"After all *that's* happened to you? You like it?"

"You haven't an inkling of what all has happened to me. I need to get off the line, though. I'm expecting another call. Good night, Shelby." She hung up the phone.

## nineteen

Erik's call didn't come until almost nine, but time had ceased to matter. Her heart was soaring.

"I got a message here you wanted me to call," his deep voice said. "I hope it wasn't an emergency. I've been out of town."

"It was sort of an emergency, but it's all over now. I wanted to thank you for the verse."

"Verse?"

"In Second Timothy."

"About God not giving us the spirit of fear?"

"That's the one."

He paused. "Something did happen. What is it, Clarette? What happened? You sound different. No, never mind. Not on the phone. Put the coffee pot on, I'll be right over."

By the time his knock sounded, the percolator was chuckling on the stove and the pleasant aroma of coffee filled the kitchen. He pulled her into his strong arms and held her tightly to him. "I'm so sorry I wasn't here."

"It's all right. Don't apologize."

He stepped back and looked at her. "What did they do? Did they hurt you?"

She took him by the hand and led him to the table. He looked at her open Bible lying there. "What's this?" The blue eyes searched her face. She turned to the flyleaf and showed him the words she'd written only a few hours earlier.

"You've asked Jesus into your heart? But that's wonderful news. I thought you were hurt. I thought. . ."

"Sit down and I'll tell you everything."

As they sipped cups of coffee she told him the story, even

including the details of Shel's involvement with the Klan and his warning for her to get out of town. He gave grunts and nods and looks of surprise as she talked.

"I've never known such awful fear," she said after the story was all told. "But the fear of not knowing what would happen to me if they killed me was worse. I had to find out how I could know for sure."

"You went to the right place. Mama Sue knows what it's like to stare death in the face. And she knows Jesus!"

"And now I know Him too, and I feel so clean. I feel like I've had a bath on the inside of me."

His deep laughter filled the room. She'd never heard him laugh out loud before. "I've never heard it put quite like that, but it's true." He reached across the table for her hand. "I talked to my father today. I told him about the harassment you've received here. Since local officials won't do anything to stop this, he suggested we turn to the Feds. He knows the men to talk to in Oklahoma City and agreed to make a few calls for us. We should have someone here to investigate in a week or so."

"Now that's good news. I'd like to at least be able to go to town without fear of being grabbed by hooded men."

He squeezed her hand. "If I have to go out of town again, I'll just take you with me."

"Sounds like a good idea to me. Now you'd better scoot out of here before all the neighbors start talking."

At the door, he turned to hold her once more. "Clarette, I feel like my heart is about to explode. I've been praying. . ."

"You and my grandmother in New York. Goodness sakes, I didn't have a chance."

"Next Saturday I'd like the pleasure of taking you to Swan Lake for a picnic." He stroked her hair. "Would you go with me?"

"I'd love to go. May I bring my Bible? I have so many questions."

"Bring it. I'm not sure I can answer them all, but I'll try." He kissed her nose lightly and was gone.

The next morning she called Grandmother Vanderpool and told her the good news, then she called Herta to tell her to find a new roommate and to ship the rest of her belongings to Tulsa. It was a decisive move, but one that made her feel wonderful. Better even than the day she'd been hired on at the *New York American*.

She stayed home for the next few days, just to be cautious. She wasn't sure how she'd know when the federal officials had done their job, but surely Erik would let her know. She spent her days absorbed in her writing.

Finally, on Friday, she felt surely it would be safe to venture out again. She needed to go to the grocery to purchase items for their picnic the next day. And now she had several articles that needed mailing.

She was excited about the plans to spend a quiet day together with Erik. She remembered his first kiss when they had been wading in the stream up in the hills. How that kiss had puzzled her! But she was puzzled no longer. Since she'd asked Jesus into her heart, Erik seemed so different. For that matter, everything seemed different.

Back at her apartment was her half-written letter to her mother asking for forgiveness for her actions through the years. It was difficult to write. She had always thought of her family as being full of pride, but now she could see she was just as prideful as they, but in a different way. Proud of her own independence, proud of all her accomplishments. Never could she remember having thanked her parents for their love to her. The grief she'd caused them weighed heavy on her heart. Hopefully the letter would make everything right again. Already she felt better about it.

She gazed up at the sky. It had never looked bluer, and the puffy summer clouds had never been whiter. Not even the stifling Oklahoma heat could put a damper on her soaring spirits.

Suddenly, the sound of squealing brakes made her freeze in fear. A black touring car stopped beside her a full block from the trolley stop. She turned to run, but it was too late. The hooded men leaped from the car and grabbed her, thrusting her into the car.

"Girlie, you are one dumb dame." He thrust the newest issue of *Mosaics* in her face—the issue she'd not even seen yet. "We kill people for less than what you've done in this town." As he talked, the other man in the back seat blindfolded her and tied a dry gag around her mouth. "You've been warned. Now it's time to show you we mean business."

She never should have come out alone. She should have waited. Waited until Erik could be with her, or waited until the federal officers had come. Now it was too late. She winced as her hands were bound tightly behind her back. *"God hath not given us the spirit of fear. . ."* her mind recited.

The car was driving out of town, she could tell by the dust and the bumpy roads—much farther than the other time. After a long painful ride, the car stopped and she was taken inside a house. The stench of tobacco and whiskey filled the room where they placed her.

"Now, sister, you wait in here with your friend, and we'll see you at the party tonight."

She was led to a far wall and made to sit on the floor. Thankfully the gag was removed, but the blindfold stayed in place. After the door closed, she heard a soft voice. "That you, Miss Clarette?"

She recognized the voice. "Preacher Sam? Why are you here?"

"Oh they got they reasons. You know how they is. Empty-headed thinking. They say I's the reason you got your stories."

"No! They couldn't! That's not true." She wiggled and squirmed trying to get loose. Eventually she was able to lean over to her buckled knees and push the blindfold up and off her face. Preacher Sam was sitting in a straight-back chair with his hands tied behind him. She studied every detail of the small bedroom. Lamps, curtains, bureau, even the pictures on the wall. If she survived this, she wanted to come back here and bring officers with her.

Into the late afternoon, Preacher Sam prayed and recited scriptures, which comforted Clarette in a way she'd never thought possible.

Finally, after dark, hooded figures came in to take them out. This time, no one spoke. Her blindfold was replaced. She heard Preacher Sam gasp as he was pushed into the back seat of the long touring car. They put her in the front seat between two hooded men.

The drive was winding and upward. She had no idea how far out of the city they were. She thought she could hear the sounds of other cars. Suddenly the car turned and dipped as though going through a ditch; from there the ride was much rougher— probably through a field. Then the car lurched to a halt.

The blindfold was taken from her eyes and the sight before her made her blood run cold. The hillside was filled with hooded figures standing in a circle around flaming crosses atop the hill. Each person held a flaming torch. An endless line of cars, with headlights glowing, was parked nearby to add light to the orange flames dancing and leaping from the torches.

"You've been given plenty of warnings to leave this town," the man said who was pushing her ahead of him. "Since you're so dumb and hard-headed, we're gonna beat a little sense into you. Then we're gonna take care of your mouthy nigger friend here."

"But he didn't. . ."

"Shut up, yankee." A hard shove made her stumble forward and fall down into the grass. Powdery dust filled her mouth and choked dry in her throat. "Your time of talking is over."

Rough hands jerked her to her feet and a cry of pain escaped her lips. Nearby she could hear Preacher Sam softly saying, "Forgive 'em, Lord. Forgive 'em."

Her hands were untied from behind her back, her arms stretched around the rough bark of a tree, and her hands retied. The bark dug at the inside of her arms and the side of her face. She struggled to pull loose, but the pain in her wrists was excruciating.

"Nothing you can do to us will stop the truth that's already spread across this nation," she said with a force that shocked even her.

A loud crack sounded behind her. It had to be the sound of a whip. Although she'd never heard that sound before, it was unmistakable. Suddenly she thought of the lashes Jesus took on his bare back and she wept. "You understand, Jesus. Help me, please."

The first crack was on the back of Preacher Sam and he cried out in agony. A cheer rose up from the vast mob and filled the night air. She bit her lip as she waited her turn. Within moments the sharp crack sounded closer and closer. Then in a flash, the monstrous bolt of pain came down on her back as though lightning had struck. She screamed.

In the distance another crack sounded, but it wasn't a whip. It was a rifle. "Federal Officers!" yelled a voice through the trees. "Everyone stay where you are!"

But the crowd broke into a frenzy, scattering like leaves in an autumn windstorm. Sounds of slamming car doors echoed through the hills, along with the roar of hundreds of motors.

Through the trees, Clarette could make out a hooded figure running toward her. One straggler, probably sent back to finish her off so she couldn't testify against them.

"Clarette!" He was yanking off the hood. It was Erik! "Clarette, thank God you're alive." He was cutting the ropes. Their bite let go of her aching wrists. His face through the dim light of the still-burning crosses was the most beautiful sight she'd ever seen.

"Erik," she whispered through the veil of pain, "how did you know?"

Another hooded figure was cutting the ropes that held Preacher Sam. "*I* told him," the other man hollered as he gently laid Preacher Sam down on the grass. "Me—the great hero!" Shelby yanked off his hood.

"Shel! Oh thank you, Shel."

"He finally came through," Erik said to her. The white-hot pain in her back was heightening as he pulled off his white robe and wrapped her in it. He held her close and kissed her face. "I love you, Clarette. I almost went crazy when I found out they'd taken you."

Her mind was fuzzy. "Where are the federal officers?" she asked. She wanted to tell them everything before it escaped her mind.

"They aren't coming until tomorrow," he told her as he cradled her in his arms.

"But I heard. . ."

"That was Gaven. Has a great voice for such a little guy, don't you think? Really made them scatter. I'm sorry we didn't get here in time. We came as fast as we could after Shel finally decided to squeal."

"You was on time," Preacher Sam said. "We's both alive. I calls that being right on time."

The silver Kissel came bumping through the trees toward them with Gaven at the wheel.

"It's going to be a painful ride to the hospital," he told her, but at that blessed moment she passed out cold.

# twenty

"She'll carry the scar for the rest of her life." The soft female voice was coming through a fog. Clarette was lying on her side and the voices were behind her.

"I understand there's to be a federal investigation."

"There should be. This is a terrible indictment on our city."

Clarette forced her eyes open. The whiteness of the room made her squint. A curtain was drawn partially around the bed. "Erik? Where's Erik?"

Steps came around the bed and she looked up into the face of a matronly nurse. "Your young man named Erik is waiting out in the hallway till we get this terrible wound dressed."

A fresh wave of pain washed over her as the bandages were applied. The nurse took her hand, and Clarette squeezed with all her might. "Where's Preacher Sam? The black man who was with me out there? Is someone taking care of him?"

The nurse gave a soft chuckle. "Yes, they are. At first they weren't going to, but that big Swede was threatening to tear the emergency room apart if they didn't."

Clarette managed a weak smile. That was her Erik! It was a struggle to force her eyelids to stay open.

"They've given you something to make you sleep," the nurse told her. Then she said, "I'm so sorry about this, my dear. Those people have to be stopped."

"They won't be stopped," Clarette said through her gritted teeth, "until this city finally gets weary of mob rule."

"There now," said the other voice behind her. "You're all bandaged. Your beau can come in now."

And then Erik's presence was there filling the room. He knelt down by the bed, cupped her face in his hands, and showered her with gentle kisses. "I thought I'd lost you. Before I ever really had you, I thought I'd lost you." She felt his wet tears on her face.

"Don't be silly. You had me. You just didn't know you had me." The pain meant nothing now. Now that he was there beside her. "Thank you for rescuing me. Where's Shelby? He's surely in danger now."

"You're right. Once the Klan learns who blew the whistle on them tonight, his life won't be worth much. So he caught the train to New York just a few minutes ago."

"Thank goodness."

"Clarette, I love you," he told her as he caressed her face. "Will you marry me and go away with me?"

"Away? Away where?"

"Dad says they need a newspaper for the boom towns in Osage County. He wants us to come up there and start our very own newspaper. Marry me, Clarette. Please say you'll marry me."

Her heavy eyelids closed as she mused over that thought. "Our very own paper?"

"Our very own."

"And I can still write for magazines?"

"You can write all you want. As long as you write for our paper as well."

"Grandmother Vanderpool was right. The Lord really was guiding my steps all along."

"Guiding you right into my waiting arms. Clarette, will you marry me?"

"I'm so sleepy, my mind is mush. Please say you'll be right here when I awake. Don't leave me, Erik."

"I'll be here, darling Clarette. I'll be by your side from now on."

With that delicious thought, she could fight the drowsiness no longer. Her last waking thought was for morning to come quickly, so she could see the expression on his wonderful face when she said "Yes."

# A Letter To Our Readers

ar Reader:

order that we might better contribute to your reading
oyment, we would appreciate your taking a few minutes to
pond to the following questions. When completed, please
**rn** to the following:

Rebecca Germany, Editor
Heartsong Presents
P.O. Box 719
Uhrichsville, Ohio 44683

Did you enjoy reading *Tulsa Turning*?
- ❑ Very much. I would like to see more books
  by this author!
- ❑ Moderately
  I would have enjoyed it more if _____

_____

Are you a member of **Heartsong Presents**? ❑Yes ❑No
If no, where did you purchase this book?_____

_____

What influenced your decision to purchase this
book? (Check those that apply.)

| | |
|---|---|
| ❑ Cover | ❑ Back cover copy |
| ❑ Title | ❑ Friends |
| ❑ Publicity | ❑ Other_____ |

How would you rate, on a scale from 1 (poor) to 5
(superior), the cover design?_____

5. On a scale from 1 (poor) to 10 (superior), please rate the following elements.

    ___Heroine    ___Plot

    ___Hero    ___Inspirational theme

    ___Setting    ___Secondary characters

6. What settings would you like to see covered in **Heartsong Presents** books?_____

_____

_____

7. What are some inspirational themes you would like to see treated in future books?_____

_____

_____

8. Would you be interested in reading other **Heartsong Presents** titles?   ❑ Yes   ❑ No

9. Please check your age range:
  ❑ Under 18   ❑ 18-24   ❑ 25-34
  ❑ 35-45   ❑ 46-55   ❑ Over 55

10. How many hours per week do you read? _____

Name _____

Occupation _____

Address _____

City_____ State_____ Zip_____

# Heartsong Presents Classics!

We have put together a collection of some of the most popular **Heartsong Presents** titles in two value-priced volumes. Favorite titles from our first year of publication, no longer published in single volumes, are now available in our new *Inspirational Romance Readers*.

___**Historical Collection #1** includes: *A Torch for Trinity* by Colleen L. Reece; *Whispers on the Wind* by Maryn Langer; *Cottonwood Dreams* by Norene Morris; and *A Place to Belong* by Tracie J. Peterson (originally written under the pen name Janelle Jamison).

___**Contemporary Collection #1** inclues: *Heartstrings* by Irene B. Brand; *Restore the Joy* by Sara Mitchell; *Passage of the Heart* by Kjersti Hoff Baez; and *A Matter of Choice* by Susannah Hayden.

Each collection is $4.97 each plus $1.00 for shipping and handling. Buy both collections for $8,99 plus $1.00 for shipping and handling.

# ·····Heart♥ng·····

## HISTORICAL ROMANCE IS CHEAPER BY THE DOZEN!

**Any 12 *Heartsong Presents* titles for only $26.95 ***

Buy any assortment of twelve *Heartsong Presents* titles and save 25% off of the already discounted price of $2.95 each!

**plus $1.00 shipping and handling per order and sales tax where applicable.

## HEARTSONG PRESENTS TITLES AVAILABLE NOW:

__HP 27 BEYOND THE SEARCHING RIVER, *Jacquelyn Cook*
__HP 28 DAKOTA DAWN, *Lauraine Snelling*
__HP 31 DREAM SPINNER, *Sally Laity*
__HP 32 THE PROMISED LAND, *Kathleen Karr*
__HP 35 WHEN COMES THE DAWN, *Brenda Bancroft*
__HP 36 THE SURE PROMISE, *JoAnn A. Grote**
__HP 39 RAINBOW HARVEST, *Norene Morris*
__HP 40 PERFECT LOVE, *Janelle Jamison*
__HP 43 VEILED JOY, *Colleen L. Reece*
__HP 44 DAKOTA DREAM, *Lauraine Snelling*
__HP 47 TENDER JOURNEYS, *Janelle Jamison*
__HP 48 SHORES OF DELIVERANCE, *Kate Blackwell*
__HP 51 THE UNFOLDING HEART, *JoAnn A. Grote*
__HP 52 TAPESTRY OF TAMAR, *Colleen L. Reece*
__HP 55 TREASURE OF THE HEART, *JoAnn A. Grote*
__HP 56 A LIGHT IN THE WINDOW, *Janelle Jamison*
__HP 59 EYES OF THE HEART, *Maryn Langer*
__HP 60 MORE THAN CONQUERORS, *Kay Cornelius*
__HP 63 THE WILLING HEART, *Janelle Jamison*
__HP 64 CROWS'-NESTS AND MIRRORS, *Colleen L. Reece*
__HP 67 DAKOTA DUSK, *Lauraine Snelling*
__HP 68 RIVERS RUSHING TO THE SEA, *Jacquelyn Cook*
__HP 71 DESTINY'S ROAD, *Janelle Jamison*
__HP 72 SONG OF CAPTIVITY, *Linda Herring*
__HP 75 MUSIC IN THE MOUNTAINS, *Colleen L. Reece*
__HP 76 HEARTBREAK TRAIL, *VeraLee Wiggins*
__HP 79 AN UNWILLING WARRIOR, *Andrea Shaar**
__HP 80 PROPER INTENTIONS, *Dianne L. Christner**
__HP 83 MARTHA MY OWN, *VeraLee Wiggins*
__HP 84 HEART'S DESIRE, *Paige Winship Dooly*
__HP 87 SIGN OF THE BOW, *Kay Cornelius*
__HP 88 BEYOND TODAY, *Janelle Jamison*
__HP 91 SIGN OF THE EAGLE, *Kay Cornelius*
__HP 92 ABRAM MY LOVE, *VeraLee Wiggins*
__HP 95 SIGN OF THE DOVE, *Kay Cornelius*
__HP 96 FLOWER OF SEATTLE, *Colleen L. Reece*
__HP 99 ANOTHER TIME...ANOTHER PLACE, *Bonnie L. Crank*
__HP100 RIVER OF PEACE, *Janelle Burnham*
__HP103 LOVE'S SHINING HOPE, *JoAnn A. Grote*
__HP104 HAVEN OF PEACE, *Carol Mason Parker*
__HP107 PIONEER LEGACY, *Norene Morris*

*Temporarily out of stock (including HP 1-24)

(If ordering from this page, please remember to include it with the order form.)

# ·······Presents·······

\_\_HP108 LOFTY AMBITIONS, *Diane L. Christner*
\_\_HP111 A KINGDOM DIVIDED, *Tracie J. Peterson*
\_\_HP112 CAPTIVES OF THE CANYON, *Colleen L. Reece*
\_\_HP115 SISTERS IN THE SUN, *Shirley Rhode*
\_\_HP116 THE HEART'S CALLING, *Tracie J. Peterson*
\_\_HP119 BECKONING STREAMS, *Janelle Burnham*
\_\_HP120 AN HONEST LOVE, *JoAnn A. Grote*
\_\_HP123 THE HEART HAS ITS REASONS, *Birdie L. Etchison*
\_\_HP124 HIS NAME ON HER HEART, *Mary LaPietra*
\_\_HP127 FOREVER YOURS, *Tracie J. Peterson*
\_\_HP128 MISPLACED ANGEL, *VeraLee Wiggins*
\_\_HP131 LOVE IN THE PRAIRIE WILDS, *Robin Chandler*
\_\_HP132 LOST CREEK MISSION, *Cheryl Tenbrook*
\_\_HP135 SIGN OF THE SPIRIT, *Kay Cornelius*
\_\_HP136 REKINDLED FLAME, *JoAnn A. Grote*
\_\_HP139 WINDING HIGHWAY, *Janelle Burnham*
\_\_HP140 ANGEL'S CAUSE, *Tracie J. Peterson*
\_\_HP143 MORNING MOUNTAIN, *Peggy Darty*
\_\_HP144 FLOWER OF THE WEST, *Colleen L. Reece*
\_\_HP147 DREWRY'S BLUFF, *Cara McCormack*
\_\_HP148 DREAMS OF THE PIONEERS, *Linda Herring*
\_\_HP151 FOLLOW THE LEADER, *Loree Lough*
\_\_HP152 BELATED FOLLOWER, *Colleen L. Reece*
\_\_HP155 TULSA TEMPEST, *Norma Jean Lutz*
\_\_HP156 FLY AWAY HOME, *Jane LaMunyon*
\_\_HP159 FLOWER OF THE NORTH, *Colleen L. Reece*
\_\_HP160 TO KEEP FAITH, *Carolyn R. Scheidies*
\_\_HP163 DREAMS OF GLORY, *Linda Herring*
\_\_HP164 ALAS MY LOVE, *Tracie J. Peterson*
\_\_HP167 PRISCILLA HIRES A HUSBAND, *Loree Lough*
\_\_HP168 LOVE SHALL COME AGAIN, *Birdie L. Etchison*
\_\_HP171 TULSA TURNING, *Norma Jean Lutz*
\_\_HP172 A WHISPER OF SAGE, *Esther Loewen Vogt*

## Great Inspirational Romance at a Great Price!

**Heartsong Presents** books are inspirational romances in contemporary and historical settings, designed to give you an enjoyable, spirit-lifting reading experience. You can choose from 172 wonderfully written titles from some of today's best authors like Peggy Darty, Colleen L. Reece, Tracie J. Peterson, VeraLee Wiggins, and many others.

*When ordering quantities less than twelve, above titles are $2.95 each.*

# Heart♥ng Presents
## *Love Stories Are Rated G!*

That's for godly, gratifying, and of course, great! If you l[o]
a thrilling love story, but don't appreciate the sordidness of so[r]
popular paperback romances, **Heartsong Presents** is for you. [In]
fact, **Heartsong Presents** is the *only inspirational romance b[o]
club*, the only one featuring love stories where Christian faith [is]
the primary ingredient in a marriage relationship.

Sign up today to receive your first set of four, never bef[ore]
published Christian romances. Send no money now; you w[ill]
receive a bill with the first shipment. You may cancel at any ti[me]
without obligation, and if you aren't completely satisfied w[ith]
any selection, you may return the books for an immediate refu[nd]

Imagine. . .four new romances every four weeks—two histo[ri-]
cal, two contemporary—with men and women like you who lo[ng]
to meet the one God has chosen as the love of their lives. . .all [at]
the low price of $9.97 postpaid.

*To join, simply complete the coupon below and mail to [the]
address provided.* **Heartsong Presents** romances are rated G [for]
another reason: They'll arrive *Godspeed!*